THE HUNTERS

by

Philip Howard

To Tony
Thanks for all your help.
Phil x.

Independently Published in 2023
Copyright Philip Howard

The right of Philip Howard to be identified as the author of this work has been asserted by him in accordance with sections 77 and 78 of the Copyright, Designs and Patents Act, 1988.

The characters and events portrayed in this book are fictitious. Any similarity to real persons, dead or living is coincidental and not intended by the author.

The author and publisher accept no liability for actions inspired by this book.

No part of this book may be reproduced or stored in a retrieval system or transmitted in any form or by any means, electronic, mechanical, photocopying, recording or otherwise without the express permission of the author/publisher.

ISBN 9798390011447
Cover Design: Andrew Howard
imandrewhoward@gmail.com

Acknowledgements

First and foremost, thanks must go to my wife Linda. I truly did not believe that I had written anything worthwhile. I handed the text to her in trepidation and was amazed when she left a note on the table which read: "Believable, fast-paced, I was surprised by the ending. It is the best book I have read this year."

Also, I must thank two wonderful friends. Tony made helpful comments and corrections early on and Steve aka Jim (don't ask) read the final version, as a reader of a book, to see if there were any glaring errors. If there are, it's his fault!

Thanks to my youngest son, Andrew, for all his computing advice and for saving my life, one day, when the entire text disappeared. He also designed the cover. Finally, Andrew's son, Lucas showed me how to set up my chapter headings in a consistent manner. A frustrating task that had taken me nearly two hours to get wrong was completed successfully by him in twenty minutes.

PS Two of my granddaughters, Maia and Violet are mentioned. They didn't do anything. They just wanted acknowledgement.

Introduction

This is my third book. My first two; "Braver Than All The Rest" and "An Accident Waiting To Happen," are completely original in content. The first, a novel, is about a boy who suffers from muscular dystrophy; a life-shortening medical condition, who meets his sporting hero and forms an unlikely relationship. The latter is an autobiography. Sounds almost pompous, doesn't it? What would someone like me have to write about? Except I am an ordinary man who has lived an unusual life, dealing with the problems caused by Ehlers Danlos syndrome.
In different ways, they both deal with issues around disability. It's not surprising really. I used to be the Special Needs Co-ordinator in a college. They say you should write about what you know don't they? So, you would never catch me writing a crime story.
In fact, I can't stand crime stories. I mean to say, how many ways can you kill someone? They've all been done before, haven't they? As for the locations of these crimes; there are some very dangerous places to live where a murder seems to be carried out every week. As for the police; either we have stupid assistants who get everything wrong only to be guided by their superior officer or

everyone is blind to the clues so cleverly observed by a Miss Marple or the local priest.

"No," I thought to myself, "You'll never find me writing a crime story."

Then I saw a picture of a dead lion lying at the feet of grinning hunters and began to vent my spleen. After several weeks, as the story began to unfold, it dawned on me. This is a murder/crime story! My only consolation is I think it's as original a tale as my first two. I hope you enjoy it.

The fascination of shooting as a sport depends almost wholly on whether you are at the right or wrong end of the gun.
P.G. Woodhouse

People never lie so much as after a hunt, during a war or before an election.
Otto von Bismark

They are killing all over the world. Man is the only animal that is to be dreaded.
Jiddu Krishnamurti

Hunting works for conservation like slavery works for economic growth. A guaranteed but morally awful way to achieve a goal.
Peter Allison

As long as men massacre animals, they will kill each other. Indeed, he who sows the seeds of murder and pain cannot reap the joy of love:
 Pythagoras

CHAPTER 1

She sat staring at the image on her computer screen.
"Horrific."
"Such vile people."
"How could anyone do such a thing?"
"Oh my God!"
The list of comments went on and on. Each one was an outpouring of grief and anger until people simply ran out of words.
There were no words. The photograph showed two men posing, full of pride. Dressed in outdoor camouflage clothing, they stood with their arms around each other.
The shorter man was not smiling. He was obviously the professional who had seen it all before. The taller man, his face partially in the shade of a floppy hat stood grinning like a Cheshire Cat. He was the customer, the client who had paid for this and had achieved full satisfaction.
Below them lay the body of a two-year-old male elephant curled up like a baby, tucked
up in sleep. The mighty hunters held rifles at their side like soldiers on parade. The weapons were big enough to kill, well, an elephant. The men were prepared and had achieved. Rachel let her hand fall from her mouth. She sat there in shock and disgust, shaking her head slowly and

sadly. The last comment summed up everything she was feeling. "Words fail me". She had nothing else to write.

CHAPTER 2

Her desk sat in the back room of her house. She and Andrew had lived here for 19 years. The walls were full of pictures of their two daughters. Emily was thirteen and Jane eleven. Besides these photographs also hung images of nephews and nieces, brothers and sisters.

Family was very important to both of them but she had also wanted a career. She had waited until she was approaching thirty and had established herself as a news reporter before having children. She continued to work two days a week on the features column of the Times newspaper in London.

She turned from her computer and could see Andrew and the girls playing with their three dogs in the large gardens which overlooked neighbouring fields. She was so happy with their environment. Three silver birches stood, in the middle of the garden, bedecked by bird feeders of all kinds. To the left a large pond twinkled in the sunlight.

She and Andrew had dug it out one summer weekend which turned out to be the hottest day of the year and they finished their work exhausted and wet with sweat, rejoicing in the simple pleasure of an achievement toasted by a glass of wine.

A Hawthorn hedge, planted 4 years earlier, was maturing nicely and set the border
between her garden and the farmer's fields that stretched as far as the eye could see. A wide variety of native wildflowers swept round a sizable lawn. Her garden was a celebration of nature, a thing of beauty. It represented, in her eyes, the perfect relationship between nature and humans.
And now this; the absolute antithesis on her screen, mocking her and her partner's
efforts. She had seen pictures like this before but now something registered in her mind. It could have been the innocence of the baby-like corpse lying on the ground. It might have been the smug look on the men's stupid faces or the size of their rifles showing that the elephant would have stood no chance. She could not say. All that she knew was that this was the day she decided to do something. It was clear that complaining to herself and her friends was not enough.
"Somebody ought to shoot them," was the thought that raced through her mind and she wondered how many other people would think the same thing when they discovered the image.
Whilst she couldn't stoop that low ("or maybe raise herself that high" she thought) she was a journalist. Perhaps there

was something she could do. She picked up the phone and dialled her newspaper's number.
"Hi. It's Rachel Hunter here." The irony of her name only struck her when she said it.
"Can you put me through to Sebastian Johnson please?"

Johnson was the editor of the Sunday Times and the commissioning officer for new projects.
She had worked with him on several pieces and knew he would be interested in her
ideas. The phone rang for a considerable period but Rachel was so intense and focused it did not occur to her that maybe she should have hung up and tried later.
"Johnson".
The harshness of his voice made her jump out of her trance.
"Sebastian, Hi. It's Rachel. I have an idea for a project. Can we meet?"

CHAPTER 3

The meeting with Johnson progressed very well and before she knew it she was boarding a plane to South Africa. It had taken only two weeks to arrange the trip. This had caused her some problems in preparation but with Andrew's help and reassurance, she found herself seated next to a window overlooking ground staff making the last preparations before take-off. She had specifically requested a seat by the window as she liked reading in natural light when possible and had a lot of reading to do.

Rachel had quickly realised that all she had on this subject matter was her indignation. She knew nothing about Africa, and less still about hunting or the hunting industry. The paper had moved so quickly in response to her proposal because it wanted to catch the public mood. Stories can go out of fashion very quickly and there was no reason to believe that a competitor wasn't making the same preparations.

Dozens of emails had passed between her and SMS Safaris dealing with such things as details of the equipment and clothing that she would require, to locations and arrangements for transport from the airport to the base.

She still couldn't believe she had convinced her paper to go ahead but Sebastian Johnson had been very supportive from the beginning. The photographs on Facebook had resulted in a public outcry on social media. Numerous articles in other journals had already been written and interviews on television news had resulted in further annoyance at Hunting Safari organisations. None had gone into the depth that she intended. She would be spending a week with the hunters and the aim was to produce a daily diary for a week. Her paper had adopted an anti-hunting stance which reflected well on the publication as well as producing an increase in sales.

It had therefore surprised Rachel that the paper had managed to arrange a week's stay for her with a hunting organisation. To her surprise SMS Safaris jumped at the opportunity to present their case particularly when Sebastian had somehow reassured them that her report would be a report into the facts and not engage in an anti-hunt witch-hunt. Negotiations had been detailed and intense, given the short timescale but written assurances had been given that the hunter organisation would be given full opportunity to explain and justify their activities.

As a result, the hunters saw this as not only an opportunity to justify themselves but more importantly to advertise their operation, a display of confidence that Rachel had not foreseen. She was not happy that one of the conditions for participation stipulated by SMS Safaris was the insertion of an advertisement at the end of the article but Johnson had assured her that this would not compromise the integrity of her work.

Rachel was doubtful. She would not have the final say in its contents but she had to agree otherwise there would be no project. She knew that she would have to be very skilled in her presentation to ensure that there was little opportunity to alter her work. With all these concerns she nevertheless boarded the 17.35 plane at Heathrow for what would be a fifteen-and-a-half-hour flight. Rachel was not an experienced flyer. Apart from a couple of flights to Italy and one to France she had not flown at all. She was excited and not to say a little daunted. She had a lot of reading to do but comforted herself firstly with some music followed by a brief look at a historical novel by Phillippa Gregory. Rachel found that, despite her literary background, this kind of writing was more enjoyable than pure fiction. The fact that the stories were rooted, however tenuously to real people, appealed to her journalistic approach to her own writing.

It was also true that she couldn't face reading websites about safaris and killing until she was comfortable with being on a plane. She read the first chapter of the White Queen and promptly fell asleep only to be woken by the

flight attendants serving evening meals. By the time she had finished eating it was past 8pm. She decided not to put off her work any longer.
She typed in. 'Hunting in Africa". As soon as she typed in "hunting", a plethora of sites appeared. This was a surprise. Rachel imagined that they would look like sleazy
adult movies from the 1960s, slightly ashamed of their own content but this was not so. There were dozens of sites offering guided Safaris to various places in Africa. One site had a gallery of photographs identifying African Plains game; Impala, Springboks, Blesbok and a whole host of other animals of which she'd never heard. All were paraded there to be mounted on a prospective customer's wall even before they had been shot.
One page went further and invited readers to "Know the trophy you are going to be hunting for". To help the prospective customer a whole list of animals identified as trophies appeared. Each photograph had target spots to show where the best shot could produce the most effective kill. The text around each species gave a detailed description of its preferred habitats.
Rachel was to be the guest of SMS Safaris. In the "about us" page it described how SMS safaris had grown into one of Africa's premier hunting outfitters "with a record of producing world-class trophies through ethical fair chase

hunting". It then went on to say that they weren't just providing a hunt. "What's a complete safari adventure without ensuring the experience of a lifetime?". So, it placed the hunting and killing within the boundaries of a holiday; exploring the countryside, the cuisine and the people as if killing animals was just a part of any holiday.

One package provided shipping to a local taxidermist. Rachel found this particularly revolting. Preserving the body of a dead animal that you had just killed so that you could place its head on your living room wall seemed to be the most pointless of all the tasks, as bad as the killing itself. Humans didn't own these animals. "Animals weren't placed on this earth for humans to play with, to abuse," she reasoned to herself.

She was surprised at how angry she was becoming. She had forgotten her nervousness

about the flight and was becoming focused on the task in front of her.

She was also annoyed that she had to present an unbiased view of this.

"How could any human being with any sense of compassion be neutral about the mass killing of hundreds of animals?" She had to "obey her instructions and remain professional at all times," but if you were neutral about something you found morally reprehensible weren't you complicit in the continuation of that act?

Another option provided by SMS offered, "a hunting and golfing adventure with 3/4 nights hunting combined with 2 days of golf in some of Africa's finest golf courses".

"They'd better not get the wrong equipment on the golf course." thought Rachel. It could lead to a very nasty accident or even worse. "What if you faced a charging elephant and pulled out a 7 Club?".

She smiled but then admonished herself. She was making fun of her subject matter. If she was going to carry out an investigative piece of journalism, she had to control her own personal biases. She couldn't let her own personal feelings interfere in her work.

She realised that she had been naive to think her articles would be an uncovering of the

truth. The truth was already out there, completely uncovered. The people she would be investigating showed no hint of remorse or acknowledgement of wrongdoing. Her article was not going to be an expose.

Instead, she would be examining the activities, the rationale and the justifications of safari hunters. She had to be fully focused and aware of all the arguments on both sides. There was no room for any flippancy. She might not need to chase about with the hunters. Instead, she would be simply carrying out a series of interviews. Maybe it was going to be easier than she thought. She couldn't have been more wrong.

CHAPTER 4

"This is your captain speaking. We shall be arriving at Oliver Tambo International Airport Johannesburg in approximately 2 hours; it is now 6 a.m. local time. Breakfast is now being served."

Staff began busying themselves as lights came on in the main cabin. Rachel opened the blinds to reveal a bright and clear sky. She had slept for nearly eight hours. She thought of Andrew and the girls and suddenly felt very alone.

"Stop it." she commanded. "You wanted this, you're on a mission at the possible height of your career. You have to make sacrifices if you are going to succeed. Deal with it."

Rachel refocused and then looked at a couple more photographs on her laptop. She was so busy trying to absorb herself in her preparations that she was surprised when she felt the wheels bump on the tarmac. She had arrived. Rachel quickly put her phone, the photographs and her feelings of loneliness into her bag.

She was disappointed by the airport as she moved through Arrivals and Customs; it seemed far away from an African adventure. It could have been any airport in the world. Rachel already began to realise that Africa, as she imagined it, was a long way away. She was entering a modern international City twice the size of Manchester. Her destination, the ranch, was still a plane journey and a two-hour bus ride away.

She collected her bags from the baggage carousel and turned left into the main

arrivals lounge. The departure screen indicated that her flight to Polokwane, the capital of the Limpopo province, was boarding in 30-minutes.

Rachel still had a long journey ahead of her. Undaunted, she boarded the plane. Excitement began to creep over her and her spirits were beginning to lift. The nervous girl, initially unsure of herself, was beginning to emerge into an intrepid reporter who did not read or watch the on-board movie. Instead, she was entertained by the unfolding vision below her as the city gave way to countryside, to farms and eventually to a more untamed, huge vista of shrub and bushland.

She was beginning to enjoy herself and relax when an array of buildings denoting the outlying districts of Polokwane appeared on the horizon. Within minutes the plane landed and she prepared to disembark.

Rachel took her luggage from the carousel. She recognised him immediately from the photograph that SMS safaris had sent to her. Kyle was about 6'2" tall, well-tanned and athletically built. He was holding a placard with her name on it. She blinked at the

realisation of the irony of her surname. It had not occurred to her. "Hazel Nut,", she
thought to herself. He had a winning smile and gentle eyes, not what she had expected from a professional hunter whom she had expected to dislike from the outset.
"Mrs Hunter?"
"Ms" she corrected.
"Sorry I'm Kyle from s SMS safaris. I've come to collect you. You were expecting me?"
"Yes. I had your name and a photograph."
"Good, here's my card." He handed it over to her for safekeeping. It read "Kyle Johansen, professional hunter". The text centred around a photograph of some animal she could not identify despite having studied the pictures on the website; the ones with the rifle target pointed at the best position for the most efficient kills.
"Shall we go? You must be very tired.
She smiled.
"Thank you, I can't wait to get there."
"We will be there in approximately 2 hours."
"It said 4 hours in your brochure."
"Really? Perhaps they don't drive as quickly as I do." He smiled as he lifted her bags onto the rear seat of the Ranger.
"Ah, that's probably talking about loading up and transporting a full vehicle."

He opened the passenger door to allow her access. She stood on the step and nimbly moved to her seat avoiding his outstretched hand which offered support.

"You must be a VIP, as you are my only pick-up to-day."

"Are you a taxi driver then?"

"No, I work for the safari. I'm a guide and professional hunter."

"Oh yes of course. It said so on the information I received. I'm a bit disorientated.

The sun was already beating down and the temperature inside the vehicle was oppressive as the air conditioning had not yet cooled the cabin. Rachel suddenly felt very tired despite her sleep on the aircraft.

"Here, have some water. You look exhausted."

Rachel drank a little.

"More, you must have more. We don't want you spoiling your adventure by becoming ill right at the start. You need to rest and take water."

"I've done nothing but sleep and sit down for the last 14 hours."

"It is still very tiring and it is very hot. You need to drink."

They turned left out of the airport and were soon travelling on a single lane highway that

looked as if it had been newly laid.

"This town is Polokwane, the capital town of Limpopo. It has a population of about
130000 people. I say about, because my brother's wife is about to give birth any day
now." He grinned. "The area of Limpopo is the home of the Behone people. He glanced
across at her. Rachel was fast asleep and had not heard a single word he had said.
She began to stir slowly at first and then quickly when she realised that her surroundings had changed dramatically. The Ranger turned off the main highway which disappeared quickly as they drove along a dirt track surrounded by mountains on either side. The dry soil was peppered by bushes and the vehicle left a dust cloud as it weaved its way between them.
She sat bolt upright when she caught sight of three giraffes ambling along some two hundred yards away. At the top of the ridge several pairs of horns moved in and out of bushes. They belonged to animals she could not identify despite all the hours of preparation she had spent researching her trip.
'Kudu," Kyle said, recognizing her struggles.
"Don't worry. You get to know them very quickly."
"They are very close to the road, aren't they? Do they cause problems?'

"No, the road causes problems for them although problems are actually very rare. People know the animals are nearby. They drive slowly. You don't want to hit a giraffe," he smiled. "Anyway, the animals know to stay away from the road. They don't normally come near. You're lucky to see the giraffes so soon."
"You don't go shooting near here?"
"It's another 10 km to the reserve."
'I'm not doing any shooting. I'm doing a revision of the website. I'm writing articles and taking photographs."
This was not a lie but it wasn't quite the truth. It was the cover that had been agreed with the owners who did not want their customers to feel that they were being judged by a journalist.
'It takes all kinds of people to enjoy themselves here. You'll enjoy the experience. It's a good place."
The well-sprung Ranger glided along the bumpy track and they made good progress until they came to a narrow ravine which dipped and turned sharply left. Kyle brought the vehicle to a halt, got out of the Ranger and walked forward 20 yards. He bent down and lifted two large rocks out of the road and threw them to the side. He looked at Rachel and smiled before clambering back inside the vehicle. They proceeded through the ravine and began to climb a narrow path ordered by rocks on the right and a significant drop to the left. The track rose steadily for a

few minutes and Rachel was beginning to feel a little uncomfortable as the drop on her side became more and more significant. Her hand began to hurt due to the strong grip she had been exerting on the grab handle. It was impossible not to be impressed by the beautiful scenery unfolding before her as the road reached its peak. Shrubs and grasses covered the land and small hills rolled on towards distant mountains. Kyle stopped the vehicle and Rachel gasped. "The brochures weren't exaggerating." she whispered, "It's stunning."

"Yes, it is. It is very beautiful; it makes you want to stay. There's the ranch."

Towards her left the view opened up onto a plain covered by dry light brown grasses.

In the middle stood a stockade consisting of several buildings with mud walls and thatched roofs linked together by stone walls approximately 8 ft high. Rachel smiled. She smiled all the way to the entrance.

CHAPTER 5

They passed through the gates and turned right into a parking area containing four Land Cruisers of a similar type to the one they were travelling in.
 "How many people do you cater for? "
"It varies. Sometimes we have 5 or 6, sometimes up to 15 people."
"You need a lot of staff to guide people."
"Yes indeed, we have to make certain the customers are safe at all times."
Four black members of staff served glasses of wine to her and several other travellers who had arrived earlier. A white couple who appeared to be in charge, emerged from the kitchen. The man came across to Rachel immediately and introduced himself.
Hi I'm Zach Baas, I'm the owner of SMS safaris. Welcome."
He introduced his wife, Mary. Neither of them looked like the image of hunters Rachel had developed in her head. Zach was in his mid 50s overweight and balding. He looked like a day's hunting would have killed him. "It would certainly do him some serious harm," she thought to herself. Rachel was already learning that hunters, if that's what they should be called, did not fit into any

particular stereotype. Mary looked to be some years younger. She was short and petite and looked like she could have been the owner of a caravan park instead of a hunting organisation.

Rachel was introduced to several smiling faces whose names she immediately forgot. The day had spun round in a moment. She was tired, dirty and hungry.

'Forgive me, you must be tired. You are in room 4. Please, I'll show you to your room.

They entered her room and Zach showed her the facilities.

"We rise tomorrow at 6 a.m. That's always late on the first day. The clients will be sorting out their equipment and we can talk about what you will do; if that is alright with you? Tonight, we have a meal at 6 p.m. in our main room. It's easy to find; it's not a big place" he smiled. "After the meal I do a welcome talk and explain the itinerary for the week. Then we relax and make friends, OK?"

"Fine. I'm really hungry."

"Would you like me to fetch something now?"

"No, I'm fine. I'll take a shower, thanks.

"OK. See you later." He smiled and left.

A wooden framed window looked out onto an inner courtyard where she could see a fire pit surrounded by garden furniture. She watched staff setting up tables for the evening meal then closed the blinds. It was very quiet and home felt far away. Rachel looked at her watch. She

had an hour to get ready. After skyping Andrew and the kids to let them know that she was safe Rachel made herself a lemon tea and sat cross-legged on the bed taking in the atmosphere. It was calm and restful and all her initial fears about the journey and her feelings of loneliness began to drift away. The alarm on her phone sounded promptly. She had allowed herself a half hour rest and had not meant to fall asleep. The light was already beginning to fade and she wondered what time it went dark. She showered quickly and went into the dining room where guests had already gathered.
"A glass of wine?" One of the waitresses asked.
"Oh, that would be lovely. Thank You."
"Red or white?"
"White please." She liked red but it always gave her a bad hangover and that was something she could definitely do without on this trip.
She turned around and was immediately approached by the only other female guest.
"Hello, I'm Anne," she squeaked. Immediately she cleared her throat.
"Sorry," she said in a stronger voice. "It's a bit daunting isn't it, being the only woman."
They are so loud, aren't they?"
"I don't know. I've only just got here."
Just then a trio of men guffawed.

"I see what you mean."
"That's my husband David. We are here together. A bit of bonding if you like. I've never done any hunting."
"Really?"
"No. Have you?"
Rachel repeated the story she'd told Kyle earlier.
"Oh, how interesting."
"Didn't they have anyone in Africa to do the website?"
"Ah good question" she thought to herself. She hadn't thought of that.
"Well A family member visited here and recommended me. So I'm here on a holiday as well as work."
Anne looked confused but accepted the story. She smiled.
"David's the hunter. He's been here several times. I had some lessons over the last couple of months but I don't really want to kill anything. I'm not keen on it if I'm honest but he likes it and I'm trying to, for the sake of our marriage." She leant forward and whispered,
"It's not been that good for a long time. He's not interested in, you know, sex. Not with me anyhow."
"Oh dear."
Anne looked at her and her eyes began to well up. Instinctively Rachel grabbed her hand. It looked like they were the best of friends but in truth Rachel just wanted to shut her up. She was not ready to be a mother confessor to somebody she hardly knew in the middle of the African

bush. She hoped Anne wasn't going to cling on to her for the entire trip.

"Shall we sit down?"

They sat at the end of a long table and immediately the others joined them as if they had been waiting for permission to sit down. Including the hosts, the party numbered twelve. Most of them appeared to be experienced hunters and their conversations centred around previous experiences. Anne was correct. They were loud. In fact, they were very loud and got louder as the evening progressed. For the time being, Rachel was forced into Anne's company. David, her husband, was a large man. At 6' 3" and she guessed, 19 stone, he dominated Anne. He displayed no sensitivity towards his wife at all and she took an instant dislike to him.

The meal consisted of buffalo meat and salad, locally made bread and roasted potatoes. Zach was at pains to point out that the meat was from a kill on one of their hunts.

"Nothing goes to waste here."

Rachel had to admit the meat was delicious.

Afterwards the group congregated outside in the courtyard around the fire pit she had seen from her window but now it was glowing and it lit up the whole yard. Despite its warmth she shivered and was surprised at how cold it was getting.

Zach welcomed everyone to the safari and wished them a good week's hunting. "Before we go any further can I just introduce a guest? Rachel here is redesigning our web page and will be with us on the hunts to get an understanding of our activities. She won't be doing any shooting. At least I hope not. She's never handled a gun before!"

Everyone smiled at her.

"So please help her. She'll be taking photos and may want to talk to you about the joy you get from hunting. If you don't want to be interviewed, please don't feel obliged."

He went on to introduce his 2 professional hunters. As well as Kyle he introduced Jonathan, a local tribesman who had been a guide for over ten years.

"We'll be up at 6.00am tomorrow. The rest of the week we start even earlier at 5.00am.

We'll do a weapons check and you can calibrate your sights on the range which is just round the corner. Then after a coffee we'll do a tour so that you can get the lie of the land. Maybe, if we get lucky tomorrow, we'll do some shooting. First time visitors, you need to wrap up well. It's getting colder at night and in the early morning. Hopefully It will get hotter during the day, in more ways than one."

The men laughed. They were all American apart from one lone South African. They were white, middle-aged and carrying excess weight. Anne was dwarfed by them and

Rachel wondered how she would cope with them. She also had concerns about how the men would manage. They did not look to be a healthy crowd. Despite her distaste for their activity, she couldn't help feeling concerned for their well-being. Were they trying to recapture their youth? Could they deal with the stresses and strains they were putting on themselves? Were they trying to prove something to themselves and each other?

As each one departed to their rooms, she felt a sense of foreboding and hoped it was misplaced.

Only Rachel and Kyle remained. The fire was beginning to die down but still held enough warmth to combat the increasing chill if they sat close enough to it.

"Do you ever worry that some of your guests may not be up to it?" she asked.

He laughed. "Yes, I suppose so. They are men of a certain age generally and many are not very fit. We do look after them. They don't do too much chasing about. We drive them most places. It's not like they are on their feet for hours."

"So, it's not real hunting then?"

He grinned.

"They enjoy it." he replied.

For a while they were silent. She was lost in her thoughts admiring the starlit sky.

"What are those noises?"

"Cicada insects."

"Wow. They don't half make a noise."

"There are a few owls around as well. There's all kinds of birds here. It's a bird watcher's paradise. There's so much to see. This time of year is a really good time to visit. I mean all times of year are good but some are better than others."

"Why is now a good time?"

"Well, we are moving into the dry season. Our winters are dry. It's not as lush and the animals are easy to see."

"And hunt?"

"Of course."

"When it's the wet season in October to March it's also hot and it can get uncomfortable sometimes. The bush becomes very dense and it can be dangerous. Now we still have good vegetation but it's starting to turn. Water holes start to dry up and the wildlife starts to congregate near the river. We know where they are.

We are very lucky. It's a great place to live and just as good to visit. It's so varied. The great Limpopo River is to the north, not too far away. In some places it is hilly with a forest of Mopane trees. In other places it is flat savannah with huge Baobab trees. There's Waterbuck, Kudu and Nyala." He spoke in a whisper, as if in awe, as his hands described vast areas.

"It is magnificent."

He was in awe of it. Rachel smiled.
"I'm sorry. Am I boring you?"
"No, not at all. You are obviously in love with it".
He smiled. "Tell me when to shut up."
He got up as he sought another beer from the table.
"Do you want any more wine?"
"No, I'm fine."
He sat down beside her.
"So how did you become a hunter then?"
"My dad took me out, shooting birds and rats. As I got older, we took on bigger game. We'd be out from dawn until dusk, mainly on foot, walking the bush; eating, resting, hunting. We had wonderful days out together." He fell silent.
After an awkward pause she asked,
"Is he still with you?"
Kyle shook his head.
"I was 15. I came home from school to our farm. My dad was dead in the barn, my mum on the porch. They'd been shot by robbers."
He fell silent again.
"I'm so sorry."
"They never caught them. I was called up to the army when I was 18, After two years I joined up for another ten. I then left and put my shooting skills and jungle knowledge to use here. It seemed logical".

They sat in silence listening to the sounds of the bush. The mighty hunter was a man with a history. He was human and not the stereotypical brute she'd painted in her head. She felt guilty.

"I love the peace of night," she said,

"It's not that peaceful out there. There's hunting and stalking going on as we speak but I know what you mean. It truly is beautiful. Anyway, we need to go to bed; early start tomorrow."

With that he got up abruptly as if he'd revealed too much of himself and bade her goodnight. Rachel returned to her room but before she left the courtyard she turned to stare at the sky. Millions, if not billions of stars twinkled down on her. It was so peaceful that she forgot her forebodings about what tomorrow would bring. She smiled at its beauty. She wanted to touch it, to thank it even. It was a strange feeling of appreciation and gratitude. She turned towards the building and acknowledging the notice which said, 'Please keep this door locked at all times,' she duly made sure it was shut. Rachel entered her room, changed into a cool, light nightdress and was asleep before her head hit the pillow.

CHAPTER 6

She awoke to the sound of gunfire. It was alarming at first until she realised that it came from the range where some of the party were busy testing their equipment. Some had more work to do than others. Whilst most of them had brought their own rifles, a couple were busy familiarising themselves with the rifles they had hired from their hosts. It was possible to hire a rifle for the week and avoid the hassle of getting your own guns through customs control but guns were like any other tool; you had to get used to them.

Rachel dressed and stumbled down to a quick coffee and light breakfast.

She sat down and immediately Anne entered, poured herself a coffee and sat down opposite her.

"Did you sleep OK?"

"Yes, thanks. Did you?"

"Yes, surprisingly. I spent a lot of time asleep yesterday but it didn't stop me sleeping all night."

Anne smiled.

"We're going on a tour aren't we? If we get lucky, we may do some shooting. David's really excited. He's been out practising."

"Haven't you?"

"Er, no. I'll be fine."
"Are you looking forward to today?"
"Yes, I think so."
"Only think so?"
"Well. I'll tell you later. I'm just nervous. That's all."
She smiled. Rachel couldn't work out what her true emotions were. It would be interesting to watch her as the week progressed.
Anne gave the impression that she was a frightened little housewife desperate to save her marriage. On the one hand she wanted to help her, on the other she wanted to avoid any involvement at all.
Anne asked her what was wrong with the old website that it needed redesigning. Rachel spun her a story that the old one contained too many static images. A better website would have videos showing action, the enjoyment of the hunt and the victory of the hunter. Rachel amazed herself. She sounded like she almost believed it. They left to get their coats. Anne picked up a rifle, Rachel picked up a camera. Neither was convinced in what they were doing.

CHAPTER 7

They left at around seven. They were well wrapped up but after three hours the sun was beginning to warm the land considerably. This was supposed to be a preparation day. They visited water holes to see what game was around. At some holes the viewing was done in the open, behind bushes and shrub. At others they sat in man-made hides erected near the water hole.

"Do you simply wait in here until something comes for a drink and then shoot it?"

Kyle laughed. "Yes, that's about It."

"Isn't that cheating?

Kyle laughed again, "What do you think hunting is? There's nothing fair about anything.

Building a hide is a human skill built out of necessity for our safety. Why shouldn't humans use their brains?"

Rachel realised that she knew nothing about hunting or safaris. She had a lot to learn.

"The lion won't think about fairness if it gets an opportunity to sink its teeth into you."

"No, I suppose not," was all Rachel could muster. Of course. he was right. She'd just had an image of the mighty hunter, stalking and killing, not sitting and waiting in a hut.

They saw a variety of game during the day and stopped to watch two giraffes wander by but none of the group had expressed an interest in giraffes. Rachel sighed in relief. A while later a small group of antelope passed by. Rachel was busy taking photographs when out of the thicket sauntered two magnificent rhinoceros. A mother and maturing offspring began to move in their direction. They stopped, sniffed the air and ran away before Rachel could get a clear photograph. She was enthralled by the sights she was seeing. Nothing had prepared her for the experience and she was overcome in admiration. Then suddenly three Cape Buffalo appeared. She knew that this was the specific species that David had come to hunt. Was he going to kill one of them now?

"No."

Kyle answered her unspoken question as he looked through his binoculars.

"One is too small; the other is bigger but not big enough. Anyway, our recovery vehicle won't be ready until tomorrow."

"What's the recovery vehicle for?"

"To bring the animal into the ranch."

"Oh yes of course."

"It's getting hot. We've had a good reconnoitre of the area and more importantly the amount and type of game that's available. We'll be ready tomorrow."

David nodded. This was a five-day hunt. There was no need to hurry and he wanted the right one for his wall. These were not big enough. They decided to call it a day and

return to the ranch exhausted but buoyant. They had seen some beautiful game and knew that there were some prime buffalo in the area. They would have to be patient. Rachel was pleased. She had some excellent photographs of local game animals and had captured some wonderful landscapes on her camera. It was a truly awe-inspiring setting.

She could understand what these hunters got out of the hunt, the excitement and tension when a potential target appeared. It was the kill she didn't want. It was the kill that the hunters were desperate for.

Day 2 passed in much the same way as the previous one. This was frustrating the hunters but at least she got some more pictures. The scenery was beguiling and her conversations with the hunters were providing excellent material for her article. It was becoming obvious to her that the kill wasn't the only experience to be had on a safari. The food was excellent and the evenings spent in the bar had been more than pleasant. What surprised her was that she found the group to be really, quite sociable. She had expected monsters but discovered nice, down to earth people who enjoyed what they were doing even if she disapproved of it.

She had an interview arranged for Thursday with Zach which would be her major in-depth piece. She was looking forward to it.

CHAPTER 8

Wednesday felt different to the previous two days. There was a noticeable change in the atmosphere. Rachel had arrived early expecting to be the first for breakfast. The sun was already beaming through the windows. Everywhere seemed bright and urgent. Ben and Kal, two Americans in their thirties, had made a kill the previous day, the first in the entire party. Although it had only been a small Klipspringer, one of the tiny ten, they said it had been a difficult kill. They had to wait for 3 hours on a rocky ridge until a pair happened along at dusk.

"Ben was really quick," effused Kal, "and his aim was true. It was an instant kill. The other disappeared over the ridge before I could get ready." Rachel tried to seem impressed and smiled politely. She was touched by their enthusiasm and pride in each other but unimpressed by their joy in the kill.

Ben beamed and was obviously enjoying the admiration of his friend. It was hopefully the first of several to follow in the forthcoming days.

David and Anne entered in the middle of these congratulations. David was in a sombre mood and barely registered a nod at the younger men's success. Anne fussed around him, bringing him a cup of coffee which he barely acknowledged. "Thank you would be nice" she hissed to herself but decided it was up to Anne to work on that.

"Morning,' said Rachel hesitantly. "How are we today?"

"David's worried that we aren't going to kill any buffalo. That's his main reason for being here. He wants to display a trophy on our living room wall."

"You mean a head?' Rachel stated bluntly. There was no point in beating about the bush. Anne was surprised by Rachel's directness.

"Well yes, I suppose so. Don't you approve?"

Rachel checked herself. She didn't want to alienate anyone. She wanted to find out what made people tick.

"I mean why not just call it what it is? Why be ashamed of it or cover it up with another word?"

"Exactly!"

Rachel spun round. She hadn't noticed that Zach had entered the room.

"But it's still a trophy, isn't it? The hunter has to overcome something, the animal you fear. You need to celebrate your skill, your triumph. Be proud! The men nodded triumphantly. Anne's eyes flitted from David's to Rachel's. Zach gestured to everyone. "Today will be a great day. Jonathan, our tracker spotted footprints yesterday about 5 miles from here. Definitely buffalo, one big one. Today will be your lucky day!"

David brightened visibly.

"Ah good. I had been getting worried."

"Nonsense, nonsense! No need to worry. They don't sit around waiting for us to find them!" he bellowed. Rachel wondered how someone so loud could be so quiet on the hunt.

"You must enjoy the hunt, the waiting, the searching, not just the kill!"

"He wants a trophy on our wall," Anne smiled.

The contrast between Anne's quiet submissiveness and Zach's authoritative noise was almost painful to watch. Rachel wondered how this little person coped at home with David. He was so much bigger than her; tall and heavy with fat.

"We shall see today. I am sure of it. The routine will be the same today. Ben and Kal,

you go with Luan down to the river. Some Kudu were spotted there yesterday as well but be careful near the water hole. There are a couple of large crocodiles in there. I will accompany David and Anne who will be guided by Kyle. Rachel, if you would like to come with us?"

"Yes, that's fine."

"Good, you will get some good photos of a buffalo kill and David you will get a trophy."

Ben and Kal left first left with Jonathan in a Land Ranger. Everyone smiled and wished them good luck. Rachel meant it as well. She didn't want them to kill anything but she didn't want them to come to any harm either. They had wives and children back home.

She realised that these two wishes were incompatible; to be successful and unhurt meant that an animal would die.

Zach turned to David and Anne, "Right we need to get you a trophy. As I said, we've spotted a small group. The tracks indicate one largish buffalo, maybe a bull. The question will be if it's old enough. We don't shoot young bulls with a fresh breeding capacity but rest assured the trackers are out looking. If we don't find a suitable one today, we shall go farther afield tomorrow to our limit of 50 miles radius. We will try but that's a lot of territory to cover and I can't give you any guarantees, ok?

"Yes, yes, I understand. It's just I'm very anxious to succeed."

"Of course. We are doing our best but we can't make them come to us," he smiled. "We won't let you down; just enjoy the challenge of the hunt".

They then moved to the vehicle. They collected their rifles from the entrance and the picnic basket and drinks. It was still cold as they moved out of the compound. Rachel slipped on her fleece jacket over her shirt and shorts. She sat in the front seat and Zach drove into the sunrise. They turned right up the path that Kyle had driven when she first arrived. After an hour's driving Zach stopped the Ranger at the top of the hill. Zach and Kyle got out and surveyed the scene through the binoculars.

After a few minutes Kyle tapped Zach on the shoulder and pointed to his right. There was movement in the thick bush. They couldn't tell what it was but it was big.

"Let's go down," Zach whispered.

Every conversation was whispered now. They began to move on foot with Zach leading the way followed by David, Anne, Rachel and Johnathan whilst Kyle brought up the rear. They weaved their way down the steep incline, twisting their way round trees and bushes, taking care not to trip over the rough terrain. Although she was only an observer Rachel's heart was pounding as the tension began to mount. Nobody spoke. Kyle hid behind a large bush, binocular in hand. Rachel saw the muscles in his neck and arms tense in excitement.

Two large bulls were half hidden some 80 yards away. Rachel could see them clearly. They were magnificent creatures. One raised its head and looked straight at her, its nose twitching, searching for the scent of a threat. Rachel froze, aware that any movement would be detected. She stayed completely still hoping her camouflage shirt and the gentle movement of thin branches in the slight breeze would blind the bulls' senses. It bowed its head to graze again and with it the chance of a clean shot was lost.

Rachel took a deep breath unaware that she had been holding it. Kyle produced a tripod for David to rest his rifle on and remained ready in case the animal should present itself once more. Rachel thought to herself that this was cheating. Surely the skill of the hunter was to fire with a gun in hand?

"It's too young," Kyle whispered. "It's big but too young," He repeated.

Zach looked at him and screwed his face into an image of rejection and nodded. David lifted his rifle reluctantly and Kyle took away the tripod.

Rachel wondered how they could tell its age and why it mattered.

On the way back to the vehicle Kyle explained that its age could be determined by its colouring. Young bulls were not taken as they were necessary to produce the next generation. Older bulls were more highly valued because they were bigger and had carried out the reproductive duties several times. It was a question of managing the population, not destroying it.

"To be successful as an industry the safari has to have a population worth hunting." Rachel decided not to ask too many questions now. She had agreed with Zach that they would have a full interview the following evening.

Rachel had enjoyed the meal on her first night but now chose to eat cheese sandwiches. The thought of eating meat obtained from this situation was making it difficult for her. She didn't understand why as she wasn't a vegetarian and had always enjoyed meat. Was she becoming one without realising it or was it simply that she objected to the enjoyment of killing? Perhaps she disapproved of the simple unreality of the situation she found herself in. This meat had not been produced by hungry hunters, hunting out of necessity but by middle aged, overweight, mainly American people who were rich and didn't need to do it in order to survive.

Rachel's thoughts and distractions were suddenly ended by excited whispers from Kyle. She crept closer to listen. A group of Eland antelope had been spotted half a mile away. Zach and Kyle were in a hushed conversation with David. They had decided that such a magnificent creature might be a possible substitute for a buffalo. There were two days left of this Safari. Getting a buffalo kill was not certain. An Eland provided the possibility to make certain the adventure ended on a successful note and couldn't be ignored.

Kyle decided to proceed on foot with Zach and David in close quarter as he didn't want the vehicle to frighten their prey away; they moved along the valley floor at some pace. Rachel was surprised at how fast 2 overweight middle-aged men could move when they wanted to. She had to half run to keep up. At the same time, she was impressed by Kyle's athleticism. He was tall, tanned and muscular and he seemed to glide across the ground effortlessly despite his size. Finally, they came to a halt, panting heavily. Zach pointed to hoof prints.

"Eland," he gasped. David said nothing but listened intently and watched Kyle's movements. Suddenly he crouched down, followed instinctively by the whole party. 150 yards away stood a huge, fully mature Eland bull. It stood approximately 5ft tall at the shoulder, its 1 spiralled horns taking it to 7ft. in total. The bull's beautiful fawn back was decorated by a series of thin white stripes. Lost in admiration she did not hear the setting up of the tripod. When she realised what was happening, she wanted to cry out but was powerless. The animal was a beautiful sight, noble and strong. The Eland bull stood on a flat piece of grass surrounded by a group of females with their young. He raised his head; proud without any sense of pride.

The shot made Rachel jump. She watched in horror but the Eland showed no reaction. Perhaps David had missed. Perhaps the sound of a passing bullet would frighten the beast away; perhaps she was simply witnessing in slow motion the time it took for a bullet to reach its target. The Eland jumped with all four legs in the air and twisted round in a 180° on the spot. It began to run, stopped in its tracks and fell down lifeless in a cloud of dust. Even at

this distance they could hear the thud as a 1-ton weight hit the ground.
Zach and Kyle cheered and slapped David on the back.
"That was a fine shot," said Kyle. You got him right on the spot. Well done."
David turned to Anne who put her arms around him and patted him quietly.
"Wow!" he exclaimed.
Anne smiled, "Well done darling."
"Wow. My God. Wow! I never thought I could pull a shot like that," he cried. "He just dropped."
"Wow!" I hit him straight in the heart.
Kyle was equally enthusiastic. "That's a great shot man. 150 yards and you hit him clean."
They ran across the ground towards the fallen victim. The men did so out of excitement; the women because they realised that they had no weapons and didn't want to be isolated in case a predator was watching. They came within 10 yards. There was no sign of life. Kyle moved round to its rear and shoved it with his boot. There was no response. Shockingly the animal suddenly attempted to raise its head, defying its appearance.
Everyone jumped backwards except Kyle who lifted his rifle and in one movement dispatched the mighty beast. Now it was clearly dead.

"Dead with one shot" Kyle turned to David and smiled. "Well done!"

Rachel was in silent shock as she watched. She wanted to point out that it had actually taken two shots but was in no mood to undermine the celebratory atmosphere. She said nothing. The two women exchanged looks and only Johnathan saw that both were less enthusiastic than the others.

"Well done dear" was the only praise she offered. Kyle became very business-like. He radioed to the office and asked for a crew to come out immediately. The Eland had to be

field dressed. Rachel did not want to know the details but understood that this meant removing all the inedible parts and guts before the animal could be butchered. The carcass would then be cut up into manageable pieces and put onto a truck, taken back to the centre and butchered. The head would be removed and sent to a taxidermist for treatment so that it could be placed on a wall all as a trophy.

"Right. You need to take photographs", Zach commanded. They prepared the bull for a photoshoot.

Zach, Kyle and Jonathan moved the body into a sleeping pose, placing its nose onto the ground into a position resembling a ballerina on the point of her toes. It took some effort to move the large animal but ten minutes later

David was squatting by its side with his rifle in one hand and the animal's left horn in the other. Zach, Kyle and then Jonathan joined him around the body but Anne declined the invitation.
"No. It's your day darling. I'll just watch."
"Will you do the honours?" asked Zach. "Perhaps this could go on the website. He placed the camera in Rachel's hands before she could say anything. There was an awkward silence as the others waited. She did not want to do this but had no choice. She pointed the camera and poised her finger on the button. She saw the animal's face reduced to somebody's photograph, sighed and pressed her finger on the button. She did this several times.
David jumped up and seized the camera from her. A smile spread from ear to ear as he took delight in his victorious image. Anne was surveying this scene in much the same way as Rachel was. She saw a sense of anguish in her companion's face and she could feel the same sense of alienation that she felt. Neither of them was enjoying this experience but had not spoken about it. Rachel saw her looking at her and they knew that they both felt the same.
The lorry arrived within the half hour as the mood of celebration gave way slightly to one of practical activity. Rachel forced herself to watch the disembowelment. She didn't want to watch but she didn't want to forget either. She started to take photographs, not for the website,

although it would look like that to the others but for her article.

David helped to load bits of the carcass onto the lorry. Before they had finished, vultures had already started to circle, waiting for the humans to leave. They were probably used to this activity and knew that it meant a feast for them.

The hunting party climbed back up to the Land Cruiser. Rachel could smell the animal's blood on David's shirt. He wore it as a badge of honour. He was proud and loud all the way back to the ranch. He couldn't shut up. The journey took twenty-five bouncing, twisting and jolting minutes over rough terrain. She felt none of it. Her mind was spinning. Clouds of dust arose from the rear of the truck, obscuring her view but she could not get the image, of the butchered corpse being loaded up, out of her head.

She heard none of the laughter and was completely unaware of the euphoric atmosphere and the noise generated by her fellow travellers. Even the seasoned Zach was not unaffected by the mood of celebration but he could not fail to notice the fact that Rachel appeared tormented. She saw him looking at her and immediately averted her eyes. For a moment she wondered whether he knew her feelings and whether he had any sympathy for them but he did not show anything.

Rachel began to take photographs to try and hide her face from the others but the group was so self-absorbed no-one else noticed her anguish. She kept pressing the button on her camera.

When they arrived back at the ranch Zach poured a round of whisky for everyone and they all said a toast to what Zach described as the "Mighty Eland!"

"The Mighty Eland!" cried the others and downed their drinks in one. Rachel swallowed

hers in one gulp and felt it hit her throat and roar down her chest. She then left the group and went to her room. Only Kyle noticed her leave.

CHAPTER 9

She flung the door shut and threw herself on the bed. She sat up and clasped her hands together digging her nails into her skin. She wanted to cry but tears would not fall. She was beyond tears, beyond anger even. She was consumed by loathing.
They had stalked a completely harmless and innocent animal, which had been quietly grazing on a hillside when its brains had been blown out by a group of cheering, whooping, alienated human beings. Its head had then been mounted in a pose on the floor for photographs. The site of its blood on Even now, in her room she could smell death. She could see his face; the stupid, stupid grin on his face and then they had the gall to say a toast to the animal. They even called it a noble beast worth honouring. This "honour" was for the humans not for the animal. They had called it a "magnificent kill." Then they dressed it up to disguise the reality with terms like "honour" "noble" and "magnificence." Rachel was beside herself. She got up from the bed and paced the room like a caged tiger unable to stop moving, She was panting heavily and thumping herself but still tears wouldn't fall. She was empty, empty of tears, empty of words and empty of hope. Then she fell to the floor and the dam wall burst as the tears burst forth.

She lay there sobbing for minutes. As the tears began to subside she became aware of water running and realised she had turned the shower on.

Rachel dragged herself off the floor and undressed slowly and painfully. Her whole body ached

with the sobbing. She walked into the shower which was very hot but did not flinch. She wanted to feel pain as she leant against the shower wall. She had witnessed something terrible and had not done anything to stop it and was wracked with guilt, stung by the water and sorry for the dead animal.

Rachel turned the temperature down and began to shower. The water now caressed her and as she ran her hands over her body she became strangely aroused. Her whole being was feeling sensations she had never experienced before in this heightened state. She finished showering and stepped out of the bathroom into the main room to finish drying off. She was rubbing herself vigorously to the point that it began to hurt.

Rachel wrapped a towel around her and sat in front of a mirror to dry her hair. All her movements were rapid and forceful to the point of self-harm. A knock on the door

stopped her in her tracks. Dressed only in her towel she opened the door slightly. She knew who it was before she had opened it. Kyle stood in the door frame and almost filled it.

"Hi," he whispered.

"Hi."

"Are you OK?"

" Yes," she breathed the words out of her.

There was a moment's pause.

"May I come in?"

She opened the door fully. He walked in, put his arms around her and kissed her. She responded equally, wrapping her left leg round him. The towel fell to the floor and in a moment they fell onto the bed. In one move he entered her and she climaxed immediately. As he continued thrusting she lost control of her arms and they fell from his back. She was lost in ecstasy. She gasped for air as she felt his body quivering above her. He grunted and fell to her side. They lay there for a moment only. Then he moved away from her, stood up and left without saying a word.

There was a second knock on the door. She woke up and found herself still wrapped in her towel, her hair still damp.

"Rachel, are you alright?"

She was confused and disorientated.

"Hello, Rachel? Are you OK?"

Rachel stood up and opened the door.

"Oh, thank goodness you are alright. I heard you shouting."

"I'm OK Anne. Thank you."
"I think I had a bad dream." Rachel brushed her hair back from her forehead and held her hand on top of her head for a moment.
"You think you had a dream?"
"Er, yes. I, er, well, it seemed so real. I don't understand."
"You're OK?"
"Yes," she whispered."
Anne looked unconvinced.
"Yes, yes" she spoke more loudly. I'm fine, really, I'm fine."
"Must have been a hell of a dream."
Anne waited. "Are you going to tell me what it was about?"
"Er, I'm really not sure," she lied.
"Oh well," Anne sighed. "If you want to talk about it we'll be in the bar after our meal."
"Oh right. I'm not sure. I've got some work to do."
Don't worry. David's planning on going after a buffalo tomorrow. I thought I'd go to a nature reserve. I've spoken to Zach and he's agreed to provide a vehicle and a driver. Fancy coming along?"
"Oh yes actually I'm not sure I could face another..."
"Killing? No, I'm not. It could be David's greatest hunting triumph and I've tried to join in, I really have but I can't bear it. I need to get away. So you'll come?"

"Yes."

"Oh good. We leave straight after breakfast."

Rachel closed the door and leant against it trying to make sense of what she had experienced. It had felt so real. Kyle was not unattractive. If she was honest, she found him to be very attractive. He was handsome in a rugged sort of way. She was struggling to admit her thoughts to herself. She was annoyed that she had those feelings. His physical qualities were one thing but he was everything she disliked or thought she did.

Had the killing stirred up some raw, unexplainable, animalistic emotions in her that most people never experienced and if they did, suppressed? Here they had been exposed. They were base, abhorrent and at the same time passionately enticing. She looked at herself, in the mirror. covered only by the bath towel then let it drop to the floor. At 5'5 she wasn't bad looking at all. Her light brown hair contained a couple of grey streaks and she was only a couple of pounds heavier than when she had met Andrew, despite two pregnancies. The thought of Andrew stopped her in her tracks. Guilt swept over her and she pushed the fantasy to the back of her mind.

She sighed and sat down on the bed wondering what the kids were doing now. Still feeling hot and uncomfortable, Rachel got dressed and headed for the dining room. The work she had referred to when speaking to Anne was an

interview with Zach about the hunting industry. She had spent days researching facts and preparing questions. It was the focal point of her visit and she was looking forward to it.
She entered the dining room and found to her embarrassment that the only seat free was next to Kyle. she sat down nervously and found herself unable to look him in the eye.
"Did you have a good day?" he asked innocently.
"Interesting," was all she could muster.
"Ah good. I think. I'll take that as a positive then should I?"
Rachel smiled at him, uncertain whether to laugh or cry. On the one hand she wanted to stay away from him whilst the other wanted to pin him to the table and ravish him not caring whether anyone was watching. She began to laugh at her thoughts and he looked at her bemused.
"Are you OK?"
"Oh I'm fine," she laughed quietly and caught a view of Anne watching her. Maybe she needed to get hold of herself and calm down.
The conversation between them was awkward.
"I'm interviewing Zach later on. I suppose I'm more nervous than I thought."
"I'm sure you'll be fine. You're a professional."

Rachel warmed to his kindness and confidence. She was like a schoolgirl in front of him
and she was annoyed at her stupidity. She was a grown woman for God's sake.

Just as she was chastising herself, Zach stood up.

"Gentlemen and ladies. Today has been a very successful day and I hope that the next two prove equally so and even surpass today. It is a great honour to have met a great bull like the one we met today. David, you should be very proud of yourself and I hope you will remember today for the rest of your life. Gentlemen" (He didn't mention the women), "I give you 'The Eland'."

All the men stood up and repeated the toast in unison. Rachel and Anne stayed seated, uncertain what to do and simply smiled at one another.

CHAPTER 10

They finished their evening meal and once the others retired to their rooms or seated themselves round the fire outside drinking beer, Rachel and Zach entered his office, located behind the reception counter. It was a plain, wood-panelled room, no more than 10 by 10 ft square. The walls were bedecked with photographs of dead animals, set in obscene poses and flanked by the hunters; a decade of death. Rachel felt slightly nauseous. She had to control herself. This meeting was supposed to be a gathering of facts, not an attack on the values of hunters.

"Do you mind if I record the interview? it is better than stopping to write down everything you say. The interview will flow better."

"Not at all."

She switched on her recorder and said,

"Interview with Zachary Bass, owner and chief professional hunter at SMS Safaris…. Ok, Can I ask you about your experience? How did you get into hunting? "

"I've always hunted, since I was a young boy. Like many hunters, my dad took me when I was about 12 years of age. I loved being with him, just the two of us against the world. That's what it felt like. I felt safe with him as if, despite the dangers nothing could hurt me. Then I spent 7 years in the army, developed my tracking skills before spending 4 years with the country's game management department. I worked in the anti-poaching units. Eventually, I set myself up here in 2013."

"You were in an anti-poaching unit?"

He smiled.

"You seem surprised."

"I didn't expect to hear that."

"I care about animals. I don't want to see rhinos killed for their horns or elephants for their tusks. I don't want to see their bloated corpses waiting for the vultures. I want to see well managed populations living in well managed reserves."

"So why do you kill them?"

Zach leant forward onto his desk.

"You know a lot of the anti-hunt community have very nice, naive, airy, fairy views of nature. Very few animals in the wild survive to old age. They get eaten by predators as they start to age, if they get injured or if they are a pregnant female or an infant. Now that's a real buy one get one free sales pitch!" He waited for Rachel to smile at his humour. She didn't.

"Hunting is a very small part of this process. We don't even affect the death rate.

We're not like the situation in the US. Twelve lots of species were wiped out as a result of hunting by an increasing population and then agriculture replaced hunting."

"Well, is that true? I know In America the bison population was hunted almost to

extinction in order to cut off the Indian's food supply. The hunters took the tongue, horns and pelt from each animal and left the corpses of millions of animals to rot."

"What's that got to do with me?"

"I'm just saying that hunters try to present themselves as conservators of wildlife and their history suggests otherwise."

"I don't know anything about that," he snapped. "I'm not interested in the US Government's policy in the nineteenth century. It's got nothing to do with me or my operation. Now listen. I thought we had a deal with your editor that your article would produce a balanced view and already you've come out with some crap that's got nothing to do with me."

Rachel had got off to a bad start. She didn't want to wreck the interview before it had even started.

"I have to ask the questions. You have a full opportunity to answer them."

Zach grimaced but composed himself. Clearly, he didn't like anyone challenging his view of things.

"In Kenya some species on the edge of extinction have seen their numbers rising. We have no interest in hunting animals to extinction, we wouldn't have a business. You saw yourself yesterday how we didn't take a young bull because it was important to allow it to perform its breeding function. There are places set up that now breed wild animals in order to increase their numbers. Some of these places organise hunting of their own animals and don't touch the wild ones. A lot of time and money is being spent by hunters on conserving populations"

Rachel looked at her notes.

"According to the UN 1.26 million trophies were imported into the US between 2005 and 2014. That's about 125,000 animals a year, disregarding Europe. 40,000 elephants, 8000 leopards and 14000 lions. There are only about 20,000 lions left.

This is disastrous, isn't it?"

"Well let's talk about the lion. The lion presents a real threat to many farmers' livelihoods. They are seen as vermin. The biggest threat to the lion is not the safari hunter but conflict with local villagers. Last year, in Zimbabwe alone, thirty-seven lions were killed around one village. That's half the number of lions killed by trophy hunters across the whole of Africa and when tribesmen kill a lion they cut off its right paw and carry it about as proof of a killing. Do we still do stuff like that?"

Rachel was about to say, "No you stick their heads on walls in people's houses," but she left that for the moment. "I understand why tribes people do it. The lion can be a real problem but aren't there schemes in various countries to deal with that?"

"There are some yes but it still doesn't mean the lion isn't a danger that needs to be controlled. It is very easy to be sentimental about the lion."

"I understand but isn't there a scheme in Tanzania where tribes people have been employed to protect lions? The Government pays people to protect the lion and helps villagers strengthen stockades because they can see that lions have a big value for tourist safaris which bring in far more money."

Zach sat up in his seat. He was beginning to enjoy the debate.

"That may be true in some areas but we also bring in money and it's mainly to areas where photographic tourists don't come. They visit well-known popular and scenic areas which provide lovely photographs in beautiful countryside. Hunting safaris tend to take place in more inhospitable terrain. There's room for everybody. We provide a service."

"How many lions are there around here?"

"Well, we don't actually see many."

"How many?"

"Well, none normally. They tend to stay in the Kruger National Park which is fenced off."

"So we are not actually talking about killing dangerous game here?"

"No, I was talking about trophy hunting in general.

"So this argument about the need to control a danger to livestock is irrelevant? What threat do Impala and Cape buffalo pose to livestock?"

"None."

'So you can't justify trophy hunting on the basis of danger then?"

Zach had stopped enjoying the debate .

As I said, I was talking in general and we do occasionally get a lion finding its way here."

Rachel paused and turned off the recorder.

She wanted to give Zach a slight break in order to keep the atmosphere as convivial as possible. After a few minutes she switched the machine back on.

"Can I ask you, what do you think about the people who go hunting?"

Zach shrugged his shoulders and screwed up his face. He was uncertain as to why Rachel was asking this question.

"I give these men a good time. Hunting helps a man to become a man again in a world which has damaged everything that has to do with being male."

"Do you think men are losing out in modern society? "

"Of course, it's harder to be a man these days. These guys come here. They leave their city desks and the suits and then return to what a man should be: a hunter, a person who takes on the element of life itself, faces dangers and overcomes them."

"But it's only some men, isn't it? A few rich men. Most ordinary men don't get anywhere near this."

"That's not my fault. I can't help that. I can only do what I can for those who come here."

"It's a small minority of men. I mean if all men hunted in order to fulfil the needs of manhood, there'd be no game left. Most men would still have to find manhood without hunting? So, what I'm saying is can hunting justifiably claim to be part of manhood when so few men can participate in it?

Zach sighed, "I think so. It's what I feel."

"What do you feel when you pull the trigger?"

Zach paused for thought. He had never actually thought about what he felt. He just did it. He answered slowly

"When I pull the trigger? I feel elation. The hunt can be a long and exhausting process and the shot is the end of it. I think a lot of hunters feel the same, elation and then sadness. I mean an animal has died. You have to respect the loss of life."

"Well why kill it? "

"I love wildlife. Controlling the population so it remains in good balance is a good thing."

"Therefore, you are saying that killing an individual may benefit the whole species generally?"

"Yes. That's it exactly."

Zach was anxious to get onto the front foot in this interview. He was unhappy at having to fend off what appeared to be attacks by Rachel.

"You know safari hunts have many economic benefits. All the hunters who come here contribute massively to the local economy. About 18,000 come here every year. They pay fees to hunt and these monies go straight into conservation programmes. They spend money on souvenirs and they employ local hunters and trackers who now have a much higher standard of living. The Safari Club International Foundation says that they bring in over $400 million every year".

Rachel flicked through her notes. "According to the Humane Society International these figures are grossly exaggerated. They say it's more like $130m, about 0.03 percent of South Africa's GDP."

"My God you are well prepared," he smiled tensely. He knew he wasn't going to be able to pass off any old information as he wished. This woman knew her stuff and he was impressed. A faint smile passed over his lips. For the first time he was beginning to doubt his ability to present an undeniable case for hunting.

"Well, whatever the figures and I do accept that they are clouded by politics, we are still providing jobs for locals and holidays for visitors and a sense of manhood for men, despite what you may say."

"Is it right to enjoy killing?"

"Why not?"

"Well, some people argue that the hunters are killing for fun. Do they even think about ethical killing or conservation like you say hunting is about? They come because they want to kill something."

"Don't you think many hunters in the past would have enjoyed it? As well as providing food for his family or tribe, hunters had a high social status because people respected them. They overcame danger to feed and clothe themselves and others. There was a great camaraderie, a feeling of togetherness. All these things provided a sense of togetherness which would have been enjoyable".

"So, what is the sense of enjoyment for your clients then?"

"I think it's very similar, if I'm honest. Overcoming danger together; a feeling of joint purpose; and a genuine pleasure derived from other's success. There's also a feeling that we've helped people. A great deal of the meat is given to local villages. We take the head and the horns."

"Isn't that patronising?"

"Why?"

"Didn't they hunt themselves?"

"Most meat today is agricultural meat. We just provide a bit of an extra treat for the locals and I can tell you, our meat is much better than agricultural meat. We kill cleanly and quickly. Meat produced in an abattoir. What a mess."

He waived his hand dismissively.

Rachel said nothing. "Do your customers care about all this? Aren't they just here for the fun of the kill?

"I think quite a few of them like to think they make a contribution."

"I have one last question. Isn't all this irrelevant? Why not just use the money from tourism to preserve the game, pay farmers incentives to manage populations and avoid unnecessary killings for fun?"

"That's not really a question, is it? It's a statement of your opinion. I do hope this is going to be a fair account."

"You have my word."

Rachel stood up, packed her bag and with a smile left."

Zach sat in his office for an hour. He couldn't work out whether he had given a good account of himself or not. He sat pondering and then concluded it was too late now. He decided to go to the bar. He needed a whisky, a stiff one and a good conversation with the men, real men who understood him and what he was trying to do.

CHAPTER 11

Rachel sat up for hours. She had found the interview extremely demanding but didn't feel tired at all. She had intended to write her article immediately after the interview but hesitated. The apparent reasonableness of Zach's defence of his activities had dented her confidence. After all, who was she to start condemning people in Africa about the treatment of wildlife in Africa when she had no idea of their problems and when she came from a society which had no big game to speak of at all? Doubt had crept in and shaken her confidence and she wanted to clear her thoughts. The trip to Echo Falls would be a perfect opportunity to gain more useful information.

Despite her late night, Rachel was up at 6.00am and felt as bright as a button. It was no exaggeration to say that the thought of leaving the ranch and everything associated with it filled her with great joy.

Zach had very kindly provided a vehicle and driver to accompany them for the day. Jonathan was a tracker and local herdsman. He was over 6 feet tall and heavily built with gentle eyes and a slow, easy manner. He smiled at the two women as they boarded the bus and then hardly spoke for the one-and-a-half-hour journey to Echo Caves.

It had not rained for over six weeks and the cruiser left the compound in a cloud of dust. The terrain became greener surprisingly quickly by the time they hit the main highway.

The Caves were some of the oldest in the world and a popular tourist spot since their discovery in 1923 by a local farmer. One day whilst searching for water for his cattle he lost sight of them. Eventually he heard them and followed their sound coming from the caves. The cattle were sheltering from the sun and drinking the water.

It took about an hour and a half to walk round the stalactites and stalagmites and enjoy the Visitor Centre before departing to the curiously named MacMac falls where a seventy-metre fall plunged into an inviting pool of water.

They stopped for lunch at the visitor centre and watched children playing in the pools beneath a beautiful, warming sun. Jonathan had gone back to the vehicle leaving the two women alone.

"This is ideal isn't it? It's almost a paradise," said Rachel.

"Much better than killing." Anne replied sharply.

Rachel held her hand up to shade her eyes. There was an intensity about this woman that she had not noticed before.

"This is so much better don't you think? Much better than killing for the fun of it."

"You don't approve of hunting?"

"No, I don't. I tried to enjoy it with him but," she paused, thinking about what she was going to say next before meekly saying "I don't like it. No." It seemed to Rachel as if Anne was building herself up to say something but her courage had failed her.

"Even though I'm not with him I'm nervous for him. Frightened. That's a better word. I'm frightened for him; frightened for the animals. They don't deserve it do they? It's not fair.

No. I don't like it."

Rachel nodded her head sympathetically. "I can tell." She placed her hand on Anne's and held it gently. Anne looked at her intently. She was growing in confidence.

"I've come to the conclusion that the hunting bit is useless. I think these people are,"

She paused, searching for the words, "disconnected."

"Disconnected?"

"Yes, that's the word, disconnected. They don't feel for the animals. They say they do but it's a pretence, a self-indulgent delusion. Like, when a man tells you he loves you and then hits you."

Rachel sat bolt upright.

"David hits you?"

Anne nodded just as Johnathan appeared.

The women turned away from each other like two lovers who had just been discovered.

Jonathan saw the movement.

"Er the vehicles ready. I'll wait there for you.'"

"No no. We'll come now," Anne blurted as if the spell had been broken.

Anne slept the whole journey back which gave Rachel a chance to speak to Johnathan.

"Can I ask you some questions?

"What about?"

"You and your life."

Jonathan laughed quietly. "There's not much to tell."

"Can I be the judge of that?"

"Fine. The conversation will keep me awake.

"Are you from around here?"

"Oh yes, just over two miles over there is my village."

"Do you live there now?"

"Yes. I lived there when I was a child but when I was ten my parents moved to Polokwane. My father got a job there. He thought the prospects would be better in the city. He had a good job. My mother got a part-time job. We were much better off but I missed the village terribly."

"City life was not for you?"

"Well yes and no. I did well at school; got to university. I did a degree in the history of my people and it just made me feel like I wanted to be back with them. When I got my degree there were no jobs to be had that were of any worth."

"Why is that?"
Jonathan's hands tightened on the wheel. He sighed.
"It's still a white man's society."
"Oh, I see."
Jonathan smiled gently.
"So I came back home. I wanted to come home and I was pushed back home at the same time."
"Is that what the village is to you? Home?'
"Always. I am of the Shona people. There are others but we are the largest in number. Later my mother and father came back when they got old. I looked after them. It was my duty and my honour." He paused. "They're dead now."
"Oh, I'm so sorry."
"We all die. I decided I would continue in the village. I have some land and some cattle and a few goats. I married a girl from another village and we have two children. My brother and his family are in the village also."
As he spoke about his parents' death his voice dried up in his throat. He was a big man with gentle ways and to Rachel he seemed a little lost.
"Do you like working on the ranch?"
"What am I to say to that? Am I going to get in trouble if I say something bad?'
Rachel raised her hands.

"Absolutely not. This is in total confidence. I won't say a word. In fact, if I tell you a little secret first, it might help you to trust me."
"Go on."
"I'm not here to do the website. I'm a reporter, doing an article on hunting safaris for a newspaper in England."
"OK," he laughed.
"What's so funny?"
"You didn't seem to be a computer person to me," he grinned.
"Right. I don't want my name involved."
She raised her hands again in a peace gesture.
"Absolutely. My reputation would be wrecked if I broke any confidences."
"I did like the job at first. It was a good help to our income and the tips were good. I don't know. I thought I liked it. I think I was trying to keep up with modern ways but I don't like it, especially now. You have these farms that breed animals in order to hunt them but it's not proper hunting. They release the animals who are used to humans. The 'hunters' stand on the back of trucks and shoot animals as they go past."
"What about safari hunting?
"Well, I have hunted animals. That doesn't bother me but we hunted for the meat."

He turned off the main highway to the track that led to the ranch and pulled to a halt.

Rachel thought that Anne might wake up but she kept on snoring.

"It's too much."

"What is?"

"Too many animals are taken and they glorify it. They enjoy the killing. They are also inexperienced and not very good hunters. Often, they don't make clean kills. It's very frightening sometimes when an animal rushes at you. You have to stay calm. They don't shoot well."

"So the animals suffer painful deaths?"

"Too many times. Only last week a guy, I think he was Canadian, shot a buffalo. He was shaking like a leaf and he hit it in the shoulder even though he was only seventy yards away. The animal screamed. It was awful but then it charged at us. You don't realise how fast they can move, even if they are wounded and especially when they are angry. It charged straight at him. He was so scared. He fired again and hit it in the other shoulder. It dropped in agony. I had to go and dispatch it. It was terrible. No animal should die like that. How can you celebrate a death like that?

When we hunted for food, we shot well. We had to, as we didn't have many bullets. The animals did not suffer but this; this is not hunting." He snorted and took a deep breath.

Rachel didn't want him to stop talking. His anger was everything she needed to make her article come alive even if she couldn't name him.

"Don't they provide meat for the locals and jobs?"

"They provide meat to a community that used to provide its own meat. Now it's private property. Tribespeople can't hunt on this land. So the white man thinks he does us a favour when he provides hunter meat that we used to get for ourselves."

Jonathan was getting very angry.

"What do you think? Do you think it is right?"

"No, I don't. I don't think it is right, not at all. I wish I could stop it. They are richer and far more powerful than me. I don't know how to stop it."

Rachel sympathised with Johnathan and then it dawned on her that he might not be as reliable as she first thought. Was he testing her out for Zach trying to make certain that she wrote what he considered to be a fair article or was he genuine? If he was the latter, he must have been very frustrated. He depended on the ranch to add to his income. It was a big part of his livelihood but at the same time he hated everything about it.

"These hunters," he continued.

"Overweight men in their fifties, come and kill animals for fun! Then they feel good because they give us food that we used to get ourselves. Even the ranch is starting to farm animals so even more of them will come. This is not nature's way. It's not the "Great Outdoors"".

Finally, he fell silent. He had had his say. Rachel smiled at him a couple of times and he smiled back but said nothing. Rachel was a bit stunned. Anne's revelation and Johnathan's candid condemnation had been in sharp contrast to the enjoyable tourist visit to the caves and the falls. They had a peace about them, a stillness but she had discovered a bleakness at the safari ranch. The whole atmosphere was riddled with anxiety, tension and anger. She had lied when she told Johnathan that she didn't like it. The truth was that she hated it.

CHAPTER 12

They arrived at the ranch later than they had on other days but there was no sign of the others. Staff were busying themselves preparing for the evening meal. Rachel spoke to one of the women who had no idea where everyone was. She was walking back from the dining room, across the empty courtyard when the silence was broken by the sound of distant horns sounding from the ranch's vehicles approaching at high speed. They were still a quarter of a mile away but were clearly visible. Their wheels left dust clouds behind them as their horns continued to sound.

It was clearly a joyous parade. The Rangers sped into the parking area and came to a sharp halt. David was out of his vehicle before it stopped.

Anne came into the courtyard to see what the fuss was about as Rachel caught sight of four giant hooves sticking up to the sky in the last truck to enter the compound.

David was shouting with joy and excitement.

"I got a bull! I got a bull!"

Anne ran to him and threw her arms around him.

"I'm so proud of you darling."

David's mood changed immediately. "It's a pity you weren't there to see it." he snarled and moved her to one side before going into the bar to enjoy a toast to the bull.

He turned in the doorway and said bitterly, "The greatest moment of my life and you weren't there."

Anne shrivelled visibly from this rebuke as if her whole life was crumbling in one moment. Rachel could see that this woman was failing to keep her marriage together and needed help. She stood, a tiny, depleted figure in the middle of the courtyard. The sound of celebration could be heard coming from the bar. Only Rachel stayed with Anne, The victorious hunter received the accolades of his peers. She put her arms round Anne and guided the sobbing woman back to her room. Once inside Rachel poured them both two large whiskeys. Anne gulped it down in one and laughed.

"I didn't know you were a whisky drinker."

"Only in times of emergency," she smiled, drank her shot in one go and poured them both another drink which were consumed with equal speed.

"I told you they were detached. They kill a beast and drink to celebrate and don't give a fuck about their wives, just themselves. His greatest moment, my ass."

Rachel felt so sorry for her but nearly laughed. Anne had seemed so demure and almost non-existent when she first saw her but as she spoke, Anne became more and more demonstrative.

"That bastard hits me. How can you hit someone and say you love them? How can you say you love wildlife and then destroy it? "
She grabbed the whisky and took another slug before offering it to Rachel who declined at first and then decided to have another. They lay on the bed like two schoolgirls.
Suddenly Anne sat bolt upright.
"No!
I refuse to be a victim any longer!
Not any more!
Can't you see it's all the same?
Abuse.
Racism; violence; greed; the destruction of the environment.
They are all the same thing. It's all about hatred and anger. All these things involve; a disrespect, a hatred, a raging anger, not caring or understanding; not even wanting or choosing to understand."
Anne took another shot. Her words were becoming slurred and she spent more time thinking than speaking before blurting out,
"If you want peace and love and freedom then you, you have to fight for it. It isn't given to you! And all those fine words in Congress or your Parliament and all those people tutting over their breakfast cereal. They do nothing to

change things. All those politicians who talk about being reasonable, not going too far.
I say go far! Go further! We are not the extremists. They are. The whole world is a killing ground.
What I have done is right and just. They are the killers! They despoil the earth and its people and animals!"
Anne turned to Rachel and spoke conspiratorially.
"We have to stop them. Getting angry means nothing unless it leads to action." She waved her hands in an exaggerated motion.
"I have action," she growled. "They're going to be sorry."
"What have you done Anne?"
Anne sat there for a moment in silence.
"Just you wait and see." And with that she fell back onto the bed and fell asleep.

CHAPTER 13

Rachel woke at dawn as an early morning sun began to fill the gap between the blinds and window. She lay there for a second wondering why she could feel the sun before realising that she was lying on the sofa. At the same time she began to hear the heavy breathing of Anne as she slept in her bed. Rachel remembered their conversation the previous night. What was Anne talking about? Was she making a threat to her husband or suggesting that she was simply making plans to leave him or kick him out of their home?

She stared at the sun briefly before its brightness forced her to look away and she turned once more to the darkness surrounding Anne. She needed to go to the toilet and rose from the sofa as quietly as possible but an involuntary grunt woke Anne.

"David?"

"No. It's me Rachel."

"What?"

"You fell asleep on the bed, so I slept on the sofa."

"Oh, I'm so sorry. I didn't mean to."

"Of course you didn't. Don't worry. Go back to sleep. You need it." she whispered before entering the toilet. She

came out minutes later. Anne was out of bed and making them both a cup of coffee. They sat down together.
"Anne, last night you told me that David hits you."
"Did I? I don't remember much."
"Does he?"
"Yes."
"Have you done anything about it?"
"I think I've said too much." She moved to get up. Rachel put her arm out.
"You need to report it."
"I have."
"What happened?"
"Nothing much. They gave him a warning but he's hit me several times before."
"Are you going to stay with him?"
"I don't know yet. He's under a lot of pressure with the business and he gets angry very easily.'
"I suppose he is but it's no excuse for hitting you. Anne, this is serious."
"I know. His dad used to hit him and he's always hunted and killed things. Hitting me is nothing to him. His whole life has involved violence of some sort. He needs help."
"I'm sure he does but that's no good to you. Promise me you'll go to the police if anything happens. You said you'd take action, that they had to be stopped. Who's they?"

Anne looked surprised. "Did I? Now I really have said too much. I must go."

"What will David say?"

"Knowing David he probably didn't notice I wasn't there. He'd have gone to bed drunk and is still fast asleep."

"You need to look after yourself."

"I will. Don't worry." She stood in the doorway and said, "People think I'm weak and frightened. I'm not frightened anymore," and with that she left to return to her mighty hunter.

CHAPTER 14

Rachel drank another cup of coffee and sat thinking for several minutes. She was so pleased to be leaving. She was beginning to dislike this place intensely.

South Africa had been wonderful. The scenery was majestic, the wildlife amazing and most of the people were warm and friendly. She could definitely recommend it to her friends but she wouldn't recommend hunting safaris. Now she had to prepare for the flight home.

Anne and David were due to leave in the morning after breakfast. Rachel watched as the bus was loaded up. The two women embraced, as David helped to load the bus and said their goodbyes, having already exchanged email addresses.

"Take care of yourself won't you?" Rachel whispered.

Anne nodded. "Don't worry about me. I'll be fine."

"You must report it if it happens again!"

"I will, honest."

Anne climbed in the bus. Jonathan shut the door and with that they were gone, leaving a fading trail of dust behind them. Rachel had only known this woman for ten days but felt an overpowering sense of caring towards her combined with an equally devastating sense of helplessness. She sighed heavily.

She hated waiting to leave a place. She liked to get up out of bed and go but the long flight home wasn't until midnight and she had plenty of time to kill.
"Penny for them."
Rachel turned round and saw Kyle standing there smiling at her.
"Oh, I've just said goodbye to Anne and I'm at a loss as to what to do. I have a few hours to kill."
"Fancy a ride? I'm free now until the next lot of hunters come in tomorrow."
"Where to?"
"There's a nice spot by the river about five miles from here, well away from safari hunting. It's a very nice place."
Rachel smiled. She had planned to spend most of the morning finishing her article but there was time to finish it at home. "OK."
"I'll get some food and a couple of drinks."
He was back within a couple of minutes. They drove out in the Land Rover. The terrain was rough at first but after a few minutes a track appeared. Rachel could see the river and very soon Kyle brought the vehicle to a halt under the shade of an Acacia tree. They had a sandwich and a glass of wine and talked as freely as if they had known each other for years. It was a surprisingly relaxed occasion which made Rachel realise how tense she had been

throughout the trip. All around her people had seemed embattled, tense, trying to prove something and ill at ease. This brief moment seemed like a fleeting paradise.

"This is strange," said Rachel. "You show yourself as a man of action and yet."

"What?"

"You're so different now."

"Well things are not always as they seem. Everything changes and I don't like what's happening."

"What do you mean?"

They are talking about turning part of this range into a farm for wild animals to breed them so that hunters can come and shoot them. That's not hunting. I don't know. I'm confused but I don't think things will stay as they are. I spent some time on a farm and it was awful. They let the animals out of the pens and the hunters stand on the back of a lorry and shoot them as they run by. You have lions held in pens waiting for chickens to be thrown over the fence. It's not natural. It's not right. They talk about ethics but it's just about money and I hated it. I don't want this future."

"What will you do?"

"I've applied for jobs with the Government's protection service against poachers."

"Really? Why?"

" I suppose I've had enough. This business is not the same. It's too much and with the poaching as well It's getting dangerous. It's going too far. I used to swallow the idea that we were preserving animals but we're not."

"Good God, you too?"

"What do you mean?"

"Oh, you're not the only one who has talked about things going too far."

"Really? Who else?"

"Oh, I can't say. I have to keep it confidential. I must protect my sources."

"Mm."

Rachel was not certain she could trust Kyle. She wanted to and he seemed genuine enough, but like Johnathan before, she didn't know if he was helping Zach find out if anyone had said anything bad about his farm. Could it be that two staff were disenchanted at the same time with the way hunting was being carried out or was it a ploy by Zach? They sat there listening to the river passing by. Their eyes met and for a moment Rachel thought he was going to kiss her when an almighty roar completely destroyed the moment and frightened the life out of them both.

A huge bull elephant was standing in the track that had brought them there some 50 yards to their left.

"Get up and get in the Rover." Kyle commanded.

Rachel followed his orders without hesitation just managing to grab the wine glasses. In the heat of the moment, she still managed to worry about the possibility that the animals might cut their feet. Kyle climbed in beside her and switched on the ignition. He threw the Land Rover into gear and the vehicle was accelerating before Rachel had managed to shut the door. Luckily the elephant only pursued them for a short distance but Kyle carried on driving for half a mile before he brought the vehicle to a halt. They both broke into laughter.
"Wow!" exclaimed Rachel.
"That was a bit lucky," said Kyle. "It probably just wanted access to the river for a drink and wanted us to clear off."
"Well, he certainly succeeded."
They were silent for a minute before he said, "It's been nice meeting you."
"Yes, me too, I hope you work a future out that makes you happy. I hope you save loads of animals."
He smiled. "We'd better get you back, it will be time for you to leave soon."
And in that moment, she saw a warmth in him and knew that he was genuine but their moment had passed. Their affair would remain a fantasy, a powerful one but nevertheless a dream. They got back to the compound and within two hours he was driving her to the airport. When

they arrived, he unloaded her luggage onto a trolley. She kissed him tenderly.

"Bye," was all she could manage.

He got in the bus and with a wave was gone. She felt a tide of emotion sweep over her. So much had happened. She'd met a vulnerable woman who was no longer a victim and was planning something. She had been surprised by how similar their thoughts had been on safari hunting. She had had a brief but tantalising erotic encounter in a dream that had gone beyond any imaginings and had affected her more deeply than she realised. She had survived the brutal killings of some wonderful animals and been frightened to death by another. Finally, she had been overwhelmed by the beauty of South Africa. All this she would include in her article.

"Maybe not the dream," she thought. There was much to write about. Now she couldn't wait to get home and start.

She boarded her plane, settled into her seat and thought of her husband, Andrew and the children and promptly burst into tears.

CHAPTER 15

Her article was published two weeks later to excellent reviews. The paper was besieged by letters to the editor. Sales rocketed for the next couple of weeks. Questions were asked in Parliament concerning the importing of pelts, animal skins and heads into the UK and concerned MPs quoted her article. She was interviewed on several news platforms and also on Newsnight and the BBC's Woman's Hour who annoyingly spent half the interview talking about the difficulties of being a mother and holding down such an important job.

Rachel was nominated for the Press Gazette's Journalist of the year award and won the equivalent award in Northern Ireland. Her career was going well and she had several requests from a variety of publications to do special projects. Life was good.

The same could not be said for Anne and her husband David.

David and Anne returned to their home in the city of Eugene in Oregon. Anne felt a huge sense of relief as David brought the car to a halt in the drive. She ran into the house, opened several windows to allow air in and almost danced into the kitchen. She opened the fridge and took hold of a bottle of wine that she had bought before they left.

"Do you want a beer?" she shouted to David who was unloading the car.

"Nah. I'll have one later when I've locked away the guns," He placed the suitcases in the hall and went into the lounge. He unlocked his gun cupboard and placed their three rifles back into their clips and locked it.

Anne poured herself a drink, placed the glass on a worktop in the utility room. She emptied the clothes from the suitcases into a huge linen basket before putting the first wash into the washing machine. She took a few sips of wine as the washer rumbled into life and then consumed a few more. Anne smiled to herself and took a deep breath. She was so pleased to be home. David joined her; he got himself a beer, took off the top and raised the bottle in the air.

"Good hunting," he said.

Anne raised her glass and quietly whispered to herself "To the house".

David did not notice but immediately began talking about where the animal's heads were going to go.

"Can we talk about it later? I'm so tired and I just want to go to bed."

David nodded, but he knew that it would be a while before they would be discussing this again. It didn't matter. The heads wouldn't be arriving for a couple of weeks anyway.

In fact, the heads took 10 weeks to arrive. When he finally did raise it with Anne, he was horrified to discover that Anne had no intention of allowing the heads to be mounted in the main room. An almighty row had ensued which resulted in their agreeing to build a mancave in the extensive gardens. Anne had surprised him and she had shown an assertiveness he had never seen from her before. He agreed to the mancave but refused to take down the smaller animals he had mounted from his early days as a hunter.

To compensate for his disappointment, David had been posting daily accounts of his activities on Facebook. He had received many positive comments from friends, many of whom obviously shared his love of hunting but he was also receiving hate mail. He was used to this and normally ignored it. Within a week he had posted a series of photographs and was particularly pleased with the one that showed him squatting at the side of the buffalo he had shot. It was such a majestic animal and he felt supremely powerful for having dispatched it. He had a feeling of total control when he looked at the beast's stillness.

There were loads of do-gooder cranks out there telling him what a murdering scumbag he was. He rather enjoyed it.

He laughed at their anger and impotence. They couldn't touch him. Those critics were not going to spoil his fun and their weakness added to his feeling of power.

He dismissed them but one month after they arrived home one post caught his attention.

"I know where you live. You're going to die. The Hunter has found you." Normally he would have snorted at it and dismissed it as the workings of some crank but something unnerved him slightly. He felt something through the screen when he looked at the pulsing cursor. It had an intent and it was aimed in his direction. He wouldn't admit it, not yet anyhow, but he felt a chill trickle down his spine. The reflection of the beating cursor pulsed on his face and then the words "You live in Oregon" appeared on the screen.

The simplicity of this statement filled him with dread.

"Stuff and nonsense," he said to himself. "Anyone who has been on my page knows I live in Oregon. It's on my profile page." He loaded it up to reassure himself but to his surprise it didn't mention Oregon. It did mention Eugene but there were dozens of places by the name of Eugene in America. This person had been researching him. He was so proud of his activities that he had never thought to hide his home location but things were changing. Animal Rights protestors were growing in number and becoming organised and more militant. Shit!

They knew where he lived! He tipped the remains of his beer down his throat in one go.

"Shit!"

"What's the matter?" Anne said as she passed by his door and heard him curse.

"Oh nothing," he said. "I just got a stupid post objecting to my photo."

"I've told you to be careful about what you post. People are going to dislike it."

"I've done nothing illegal and I ain't running away."

"I'm sure that will be very helpful when somebody puts a brick through our window."

He said nothing. He knew she was right but it was too late to disappear now. Indeed, it would be impossible to disappear. He owned a construction company that employed nearly 100 people on large projects. A fleet of eight vehicles of different types carried his name, work number and email all over the state and he had a builders' yard in the centre of the city selling all kinds of building materials to the trade and public alike. It was no longer possible to become silent.

The police had been informed and had been very helpful. They had taken the threat very seriously and had issued him with a pack of information about maintaining personal safety at home and at work. Police patrol vehicles maintained regular visits to his building yard and home in order to deter any potential aggressor. Local policing, however, can only concentrate on one individual's safety for a limited period and those patrols came to a halt after two weeks.

David and Anne spoke with a personal security firm who acted as bodyguards for them both but it was not financially sustainable and after another month the fear diminished and they terminated the arrangement.

Then in June, three months after their return home, he received another communication, sent by mobile phone. The message repeated the last sentence of the original post on Facebook.

"Murderer. We are going to get you. The Hunter." They were now seriously concerned. David contacted Mike McLennan, the DI who had dealt with the first threats. Although the police were very concerned, they were, in truth, stumped. They had interviewed all known activists in the town and surrounding area and drawn a blank.

Similar enquiries by other police forces across the state had produced the same results. The phones had been used only once and provided no clues as to their location. Unnervingly, Mervyn Jones, one of the animal rights activists, had said,

"Look, officer, we are concerned about protecting animals, not killing them, not even human animals. I sometimes feel like it, of course I do. Humans are the cruellest animals on the planet. You know that don't you? Don't you sometimes think that this guy deserves all he gets?

McClellan remained silent.

"Course you do, but we aren't into death. I don't know anyone in the Animal Rights Movement who would be capable of killing someone even if they deserved it. No, you are barking up the wrong tree by talking to me or anyone like me. Whoever is sending out notes like this is trying to frighten people; they are a loner. They are trying to frighten them or, he paused, they are hunting them or trying to make them feel as if they're being hunted."

McClellan sighed. Jones was right. What was concerning was that someone putting a frightener on a victim was one thing. Hunting them was another. When a person hunted there was always an outcome, a kill and McClellan was at a loss as to how to stop them.

Next day, McClellan called on David at his office.

"I'm afraid I have some bad news."

"Really? You surprise me."

"The situation is this. All our enquiries have drawn a blank. All our suspects check out as having no involvement. We have no evidence against anyone and the people we know to be active in animal protection or environmental campaigners etc. have no history of this kind of thing. This is a real needle in a haystack and frankly we have no leads. We do have a number of suggestions for you.

"Yes?"

'The first is that you move house and ensure that your vehicles make no reference to the new address. The second is that you go ex-directory. Don't make your number available to the public. The Third suggestion is that you remove yourself from all social media platforms and finally; you're not going to like this, you stop hunting."

David snorted and then stifled it. He was obviously in a potentially, very serious situation and if he were honest, he would admit to being a little frightened. The police were not dismissing this but their suggestions were beginning to make him feel as if he was on the run. Maybe that's what these people wanted.

"They are hunting me," he blurted out.

Mcclellan continued.

"Even if you don't stop hunting you should at least stop broadcasting your activities. Oh, there is one more thing. You could make a public statement on all your public platforms saying that you've changed your behaviour and are giving up hunting altogether because you feel it is inhumane and wrong."

This time David roared with laughter.

"Officer, I know you're trying to help me and it is very difficult for you but I'm not doing that; no way."
"You don't actually have to believe it. You move house etc, keep low and then if you wish, start again in 12 months' time. This is just a subterfuge to protect you and your family.

The mention of his family made him stop. He realised it was something he may have to do. He had to protect them whatever the cost; then he thought again.

"Shit, the threat is real."

The next day they put the house up for sale and moved into a hotel on the other side of town. Within three days they had traded in both their cars for a basic Nissan. David spent as little time in his office as possible and moved between the three major sites that they were currently working on. He spent evenings at his office doing his management tasks. He still had a business to run. People depended on him for their livelihoods. Meanwhile Anne spent time at work and her mother's.

The house sold very quickly and they bought a modest but pretty 3-bedroomed house some 12 miles from the centre of town. Four months later they moved in. All phone numbers were ex-directory apart from business ones which made no reference to their home. The car was anonymous and finally he shut down his social media outlets.

One evening David and Anne were sitting on the front porch.

"When you told me that the police had advised us to move I was devastated," said Anne "but actually I'm quite pleased we did. This is a nice house isn't it?"

"Yes it's not bad at all," David replied, "and we should be safe now," he added.

The smile on Anne's face disappeared. She had taken her safety for granted and David's use of the word "should" meant that they were still not out of the woods.

She scanned the view outside the house listening to every sound. Were they still in danger? Could something awful happen? Had they done enough to protect themselves? She sighed.

Was this the way animals felt when they knew the hunter was after them? She looked at David. Had he done enough to protect them?

David was also scanning for danger. He had done everything the police had suggested except apologise. He wasn't going to do that but he felt confident that whoever was attempting to threaten him would no longer be able to find him.

CHAPTER 16

David was beginning to feel more relaxed. Business was good. The children had settled into the house. As Christmas became a memory and spring began to warm the ground everything seemed to be returning to normal and they were beginning to accept their present situation. The fact that the changes in their lives had been forced on them now seemed immaterial.

Then out of the blue David received a text message from a number he didn't recognise. Without thinking he opened it.

"Have you settled in?" was all it said.

David took a deep breath. He shut it down, then re-opened it. No matter how long he stared at it the message would not disappear. He snapped the phone cover shut again, wondering what to do but his mind was so disturbed that logical thought was impossible. He wasn't going to tell Anne. There was no point in her feeling as bad as he did. He didn't tell the police. What could they do? He concluded that whoever was contacting him was not going to attack him. They just wanted him to feel bad; to feel, hunted. They had succeeded and he was looking for a way out. Maybe he would issue an apology and stop hunting altogether. It wasn't worth all the pain he was now enduring. That was it. They were simply trying to frighten him but he was acutely aware that he didn't actually know if he was right. He hadn't reached a conclusion. He had simply created hope.

He stopped visiting his building sites and decided to stay in his office with the door locked. This was the complete opposite of his previous tactic. He realised that he was panicking, that he had no idea as to how this enemy ought to be fought. He was confused and very frightened. He tried to imagine himself as one of the cornered beasts he had hunted. Would they stay hidden and hope for the best or would every noise outside frighten him into making a mad dash for freedom? Where would he go? Would anywhere provide sanctuary? How had they found out where he was? How could they know? He sucked in a deep breath and blew it out noisily.

David decided to stay put. His office was situated to the rear of his builder's yard behind the shop which fronted onto Sylvester Street. The whole complex was sited some 200 yards from the junction which led onto a well-lit main road. Its blue and yellow logo and paintwork were known all over the region. The vehicles were painted yellow with blue signage. It was impossible not to notice Mulhern construction and yet now as he sat, working into the late evening it seemed very quiet and distant from the rest of town. No one came down this street at night.

The yard was in darkness. The office light illuminated very little of the yard as he had closed the blinds. David was getting tired. His eyes heavy as he poured over unpaid bills and timesheets. He hated paperwork. David was a builder but as Mulhern Ltd had grown he had spent more time in the office than on site. He needed to be out and about but the demands of a growing business had put paid to that. He had to ensure that costs were kept to a minimum and jobs kept rolling in. He had an expensive lifestyle to pay for. In the last year alone he had spent around $100,000 on two safaris and would have done another one had they not had to move house. He was under constant pressure and he was tired, tired of all the work and the stress.

"Maybe this is an opportunity," David thought to himself. "Maybe I need to slow down, to retire even. Maybe the police were right. He should give up hunting. It was more trouble than it was worth. He'd had a good run. His marriage was suffering. The attempt to reunite with Anne on the recent safari had failed miserably. She had tried to get involved, he knew that but she had not enjoyed the experience and now she was suffering as a result. He picked up his phone and dialled home. There was no reply so he phoned Anne's mobile.

Anne answered. "Hello."

For a minute he couldn't speak.

"Hello," Anne repeated. "David?"
"Yeh, hello. I was just checking that you were alright."
"Why shouldn't I be?"
"No reason. I was just checking."
"You don't normally check up."
"Well, I just thought I might." He was slightly irritated that she didn't appear grateful for his concern. Anne, on the other hand, wondered what the problem was. She couldn't remember the last time he had ever shown any interest in her welfare.
"You OK?"
"Yes, thanks. I couldn't find the house phone. That's why I missed your call."
"Good." There was an awkward pause.
"See you later. Bye."
"Bye."
Dave lifted the blinds and surveyed the yard. It was huge, containing rack upon rack of a variety of building materials. There was at least $400,000 of stock when combined with the contents of the shop. He left the blind up and it cast a light across to the first set of shelves. There was a considerable amount of stock. He had done well. David let go of the blinds and they rattled as they fell back into position. He turned wearily to his desk and looked down at the sheets of paper waiting to be processed and sighed. The reluctant businessman moved away from

his work and stepped out onto the porch. "Yes, I could retire easily, sell the business and….

The first bullet hit him in the right shoulder. It was an expert's shot designed to create maximum pain without killing him. He fell against the wall and slid down, leaving a smear of blood on the brickwork. The cigarette fell out of his mouth and fell onto his shorts and began to burn a hole through to his thigh. He didn't notice this. The intensity of the pain in his shoulder and the shock that sent shivers through his body, overwhelmed the pain in his leg.

He tried to work out what had happened. Had he had a heart attack? The pain in his right shoulder and arm had spread into his chest but had not moved on to his left arm. He was breathing rapidly and for the first time, he felt the dampness of blood on his shirt.

"I've been shot! Oh my God!"

He tried to get up. He needed to call for help. David grabbed the handle on his office door and flung it open as a second bullet entered his left rear shoulder before exiting and dropping to the floor in front of his feet. He heard it fall and laughed as he began to cough up blood.

"They were serious then!"

In an instant the door had flung open, bounced against the wall and closed again. He couldn't move to try and reopen it. The once mighty hunter slumped to the ground and knew he was finished. The sound of traffic and the noise from a bar across the way limited the noise of gunfire. No one would have heard the shooting. There were no witnesses. He could be lying here until daylight.

"What a clever kill," he thought to himself. David fell forward onto his knees and hit his forehead against the door he had just tried to go through. He desperately tried to hold himself against the door but his strength failed him and he slid left downwards to the ground.

He was dimly aware of his surroundings. There was a strange silence despite the noise of traffic coming from outside the yard. It was as if time had stopped and he was living in his own world, separate from anything else. Here was the peace he had just been seeking.

As David drifted towards unconsciousness, he became aware of footsteps somewhere in the distance and getting closer. They were the measured steps of a hunter stalking his prey, circling it as it lay dying, waiting to be finished off. He looked up and saw the image of his killer standing over him.

"You?"

"But why? Why You? How?"

The Hunter lifted the gun, placed it against his forehead and dispatched him.

CHAPTER 17

Lieutenant McLellan parked his unmarked police car outside the Mulhern house and sighed deeply. Officer Judi Davies sat at his side waiting for him to move.
He looked at her grimly and nodded. They got out of the car. He waited for her to come round to his side before slowly walking up to the front door. Before he was able to knock, Anne Mulhern opened the door. She looked like a ghost, as if she had been up all night. She fidgeted with the buttons on her dressing gown,
"He's dead, isn't he?"
The officers were taken aback.
"I'm afraid so," whispered McLellan.
"Where?"
'One of your staff found him at 7.00am this morning."
"He'd been shot?"
McLellan wondered why she would assume that fact but she answered his mental query with her next question.
"So, they got him?"
'We don't know for sure yet. There doesn't appear to have been a robbery. We don't have a motive."
"They said they'd get him."
McLellan was silent. He felt a mixture of guilt and frustration. Could he have done more? There would be an

inquiry. He felt he had done everything within his power but it didn't assuage his guilt nor his feeling of helplessness. The investigation had already begun and he hoped forensics would provide some clues but he was doubtful that they could help. What had struck him when he had visited the scene was the precision of the shooting. First thoughts suggested a professional hit. He wondered what clues if any would be left. As he looked at this poor woman, he felt nothing but dismay.

"May we come in?"

She took a deep breath, nodded, turned her back and without saying a word bid them enter.

They sat down in a living room and were surrounded by images of hunting. In the corner of the room in a glass display case stood a snarling leopard. On the chimney breast was mounted the head of an Oryx. McLellan couldn't remember why he knew it was an Oryx but he did. Its horns stretched like two sabres and almost touched the ceiling.

Anne bid them to sit.

"I'll just go and get dressed. I presume you will want me to identify the body?'

"If you feel up to it.'

"No problem." She left the room.

McLellan observed her closely. There were no tears and she used the term "the' body instead of "his" body. It was as if she were talking about someone else, other than her husband.

His colleague looked at the photographs covering an entire wall. Each one showed the deceased in a victorious pose with a dead animal by his side.

"Wow" she exclaimed. He certainly killed enough didn't he?

"Yes. He was very proud of his hunting achievements." Officer Davies whirled round.

"I'm so sorry. I."

"It's no problem. He was very keen. Unfortunately, others felt differently didn't they Lieutenant?"

"Well, we have to examine all possibilities but it certainly looks that way. Mrs Mulhern can you think of anyone who would want to kill your husband apart from the anti-hunting campaigners? Was he in debt for example?"

"No, not to my knowledge. I'm sorry."

"It's not a problem. We'll speak later. I'll contact you later to identify the body."

"I can do it now."

"Are you sure?"

'Absolutely." She paused. "I've been expecting this, you see. He thought they were just trying to frighten him. I asked him to pack it all in. I begged him to take your advice and publicly renounce it but he wouldn't. So why should we be surprised?"

"Did you not approve of his hunting Mrs. Mulhern?" asked Davies.

"It didn't bother me one way or another. I just didn't think it was worth all the trouble or the money." Her eyes fell to the ground.

"I knew this was going to happen. I told him."

She fell silent, lost in her thoughts.

"Shall we go?"

"If you are sure?"

"I'm quite sure, thank you."

McLellan stepped outside and phoned the local mortuary to check that they would be ready for a viewing. The officer in charge confirmed that there would be no problem and within an hour they were in the mortuary viewing room. Anne showed no emotion when the sheet was removed from her husband's head. She merely nodded, left the room, entered the reception area and burst into tears. Officer Davies put her arms round her but immediately Anne recovered, stood bolt upright and went outside to their car.

"I haven't asked her why she didn't report him missing." McLellan confided in his colleague.

"Perhaps, if she went to bed early she might not have noticed him missing until this morning?" suggested his junior.

"Perhaps" the Lieutenant said. "Perhaps." They followed her to the car and took her home.

CHAPTER 18

The investigation into the murder began by interviewing the same members of animal rights groups and other campaign groups that had been interviewed earlier. They also interviewed every known member of any group that might have an interest. Every interview produced the same negative conclusion with each person producing cast iron alibis. Very few of them even had a gun licence. Two people were found to have a gun without a licence but possession of a firearm without an adequate authority appeared to be the extent of their criminal behaviour and none of the firearms matched the killing weapon.

They were also looking at other possibilities. It could have been a professional hit. There was no evidence however to suggest he had been involved in any business shenanigans and no other potential motive presented itself but the nagging doubt remained that the shots had been very well placed: one in each shoulder and one in the middle of the forehead from close range. Despite the lack of evidence, it did look like a well-trained shooter was involved.

"What about the wife?" Davies had suggested to McLellan.

"What about her?"

"We know she had taken shooting lessons prior to the hunting trip last year."

"But she didn't shoot anything".

"No, that's true. Maybe she hated it and hated him for his hunting activities".

"Mmm. Maybe."

"There's another thing."

"Yes?"

"I interviewed the staff at the building company. They all had alibis and no obvious motive but Jane Hayes, Mulhern's secretary, is quite friendly with Anne Mulhern."

"And?"

"She told me that two years ago Anne confided in her that her husband had hit her during an argument. She told her to report it but she didn't."

"There's one other thing"

"Go on," he said urgently.

"She also told me that Anne had been for a few lessons of weapons training before the safari but she had hated it and David was annoyed at the wasted cost.

"Mmm, maybe we should pay her another visit."

"And finally."

Davies paused waiting for permission to speak but her boss remained in expectant silence.

She carried on ignoring his faint smile.

"One of the guns in the gun cupboard was a .22 Ruger rifle. Exactly the same make as the rifle that killed him, but obviously not the same rifle."

"Would that kill a man? It's small."

"It is and its light. Easy for a slightly built woman like Anne Mulhern to handle and it would kill a man if the shots were good enough or he bled to death. He was alone all night.'

"Yes there was a lot of blood. It's our best lead."

"Shall we bring her in?"

McLellan thought for a while as Davies waited by the door.

"No. Let's pay her a visit. I don't know why but I want to see the house again."

As Davies was about to leave, McLellan stopped her. "Judi!" You've been busy. Well done."

Davies smiled. This was the first major case she had been assigned to since transferring from uniformed work and she was enjoying it. McLellan's words were a great boost and she felt encouraged but she knew that there was still a long way to go.

Mclellan rang the doorbell but there was no response. He then knocked. As he considered walking away the door opened. Anne Mulhern was still in her dressing gown. She looked shocked to see the police officers.

"Oh hello. Sorry I was upstairs getting ready. I'm going out."
"We rang the bell."
"Oh, it doesn't work. I'm afraid."
"May we come in? It won't take long. Or we could come back later?"
"No, I have a few minutes. I'll just go and get dressed. Please go into the front room."
She went upstairs.
"Wow!" whispered Davies as they sat down.
"Wow indeed," replied the Lieutenant.
"What a transformation!"
The room bore no resemblance to their previous visit. All traces of mounted animals had gone along with, as far as they could tell, every photograph of her husband, with or without a dead animal at his feet. The room had been painted in plain magnolia and the dead animals had been replaced by an array of different plants. The room was light and fresh.
"She wasted no time."
McLellan nodded silently. He was carefully absorbing the changes, looking for any clues although he didn't know exactly what he was looking for.
Mrs Mulhern entered the room dressed in leggings and a light jumper. McLellan noted that although she was slight

of build, she was athletic and moved well. She looked ten years younger.

"You look well," began the Lieutenant.

"Thank you. How can I help?

"We are sorry to bother you but I hope you'll understand that we have to look at all possibilities."

"Of course."

"Mrs Mulhern, can you tell us where you were at the time of your husband's death?"

"I already told you I was at home."

"Is there anyone who can vouch for that?"

"No."

"What did you do that evening?"

"I watched tv and went to bed early, about 10."

"Did you speak to your husband?"

"Er yes ,briefly, just before I went to bed. He had been working late as he did most nights since moving here."

"What time did he finish?"

"I have no idea. Sometimes he went to a bar down the road from the yard. I can't remember its name."

"So, you weren't worried when you went to bed?"

"Not at all."

"What about in the morning when he wasn't there?"

"I assumed he was sleeping in the spare bedroom. He often did, when he came home late, so as not to disturb

me. I left him to sleep. He'd been working very hard and neither of us have been sleeping well."
"So, when did you realise he wasn't home?"
"About 10. I took him a cup of coffee and he wasn't there. I was about to phone him at work when the police arrived."
"Okay. Forgive me Mrs. Mulhern but how were things between you and your husband?"
She sighed. "Not good but not good enough to kill him."
The officers remained silent.
"Well that's what this is about isn't it? You need to eliminate me from your enquiries or to confirm your interest. I would see me as a potential suspect. Our marriage was on the rocks. I hated his hunting. I don't like guns and as you can see I've removed everything related to hunting."
"You've decorated?"
"We were going to do that anyway. It's a new house."
"Have you removed all photographs of your husband?"
"No, only the hunting. My personal photos are in my bedroom. Our bedroom. Believe it or not we were very much in love once before the hunting took him over."
She sighed. It was the first display of emotion either of them had detected.
"One last question. You had firearms training before your trip to South Africa. What gun did you use?"

"The one that's in the gun cupboard."
"Are you aware that it's the same model that was used in your husband's murder?
She gasped. "No I was not. Oh shit," She bowed her head. "No I was not." She then regathered herself. "Okay. I went for a couple of lessons in guns. You can check it out at the gun club here in Eugene. I hated it. I went on a safari with my husband and I hated it. We were subjected to death threats and had to move house and I hated it but I did not kill or arrange for my husband to be killed. I didn't need or want that. I was planning to tell him that I was filing for a divorce. I was going to tell him the day he died."
McLellan spoke quietly. "I'm very sorry Mrs Mulhern. We have to ask." Anne nodded but did not look at the officers who left without making a sound.
Anne lay on the couch and wept. She did not attend her hairdressing appointment.

The two officers drove away and parked round the corner.
"Wow. There's a lot going on there," Davies said.
"Yes indeed. What do you make of it?"
"Well, she's either a very good actress or she's completely innocent."
"That's probably been said about every suspect in history."
"Is she a suspect?'

"Well, she did say 'kill or arrange to be killed.' That was interesting"

"Mmm or maybe we are reading something into nothing."

"That's probably been said by every police officer in history as well."

McLellan smiled.

"Well, is she a suspect?"

"She remains on our list."

"List? What list?"

"Our list of one."

The fact was that no forensic examination of the site had produced any clues. There were no witnesses and every possible suspect's alibi checked out.

Anne Mulhern was their only suspect and the case was flimsy and circumstantial. She would remain on the list of suspects for now.

The list of one.

CHAPTER 19

Rachel and Anne had exchanged several emails since their return home and were even talking about one of them visiting the other as soon as Anne and David's problems were sorted out. When the devastating news of David's death came through, Rachel was alarmed to hear that the police had interviewed Anne a second time. They had formed a very strong bond despite having met for only a week in South Africa.

Rachel was doing her best to be there for Anne but was surprised at how resilient this apparent mouse of a woman had shown herself to be. It seemed that David's death had liberated her and she had recovered very quickly. She had never once mentioned to Rachel that she missed him or felt any sense of loss. She seemed to be growing as a person and often talked about her displeasure that his hunting activities had caused them to leave a house she had loved.

As the months passed she began to talk more and more about her hatred of hunting and was obviously keeping an eye on events. At first, she had talked only of her annoyance and disgust but as the emails passed between them it was obvious to Rachel that Anne had changed. She had openly applauded Rachel's article and was pleased at her success, much to David's annoyance. She had talked about public and political issues and far from just protesting, she seemed to be wanting more radical action against hunting safaris. Anne was obviously growing more frustrated at the lack of action by Governments. Rachel noticed, however, that Anne was talking about wider issues. The drunken conversation in her room when she had linked hunting to other issues like violence in general and domestic violence in particular seemed to be forming the basis of a set of political ideas. She spoke about environmental issues as well and had little time for small talk. One sentence stuck in Rachel's head. She said, "If Governments won't change things then we must and it must be done soon before it is too late."

She added "I am sick of being a victim. I won't tolerate it anymore."

Rachel wondered what she meant by this. Anne had on first contact seemed so quiet and down-trodden but her emails showed a clear transformation. "If Governments won't change things then we must" was a pretty wide-ranging statement. What did she mean by this? What did she mean by we? Was she part of some group ready to take action of some sort? She didn't seem capable but so much had changed since their first meeting. Little did Rachel know that her life was also about to transform in an equally dramatic way.

CHAPTER 20

In late August, Rachel was sitting at her desk, researching an idea that she had for an article on the development of wildlife farming across the whole of Southern Africa. Although she did not consider herself to be an authority on wildlife management in another continent, she was acquiring quite a reputation as one. She was learning fast and her relatively low level of expertise helped her in her research. She asked the obvious questions that ordinary members of the public would ask. Rachel wasn't writing from a position of authority that left readers behind and had been complimented several times on the simple clarity of her reports. Two years had passed since that first picture on Facebook had stirred her soul and raised her anger at some humans' cruelty to the animal world. She had nearly used the word "men's" but there was a small, yet growing number of women involved in hunting. One of her ideas for a later article was going to look at women in hunting. It would explore why some women had become involved at this time and explore what they got out of it but that was one for the future.

She was about to finish for the day when the doorbell rang. She was expecting Andrew and her two daughters, Mimi and Charlotte, to be standing in the doorway but wondered why they were ringing the bell: they had their keys. She bounced joyfully down the stairs and opened the door only to be confronted by two police officers.

"Mrs. Hunter?"

"Yes."

"May we come in?"

"Why what is it? What's happened?"

"I'm afraid there has been an accident."

Rachel stepped back and gasped. "What has happened?"

The police officers spoke through a fog to her.

"Mrs Hunter, I am Sergeant David Hay and this is Constable Sue Darlington. I am sorry to inform you that your husband's vehicle was involved in an accident on the M6 this morning near Birmingham. I'm afraid it collided with a petrol tanker at 11.00am. I'm sorry to tell you that all three occupants of the car are dead."

Dead?

Dead?

Dead?

The words rattled round in her head.

Rachel didn't scream or cry. She was too dumbfounded to do anything. She stood there in the hallway as the officers came in and gently mumbled other words that she didn't quite take in.

The police were wonderful. They called her sister, Catherine who came round immediately. They explained

that the bodies of her husband and daughters would have to be identified. The two sisters were taken by the police officers to the mortuary of the Birmingham City Hospital where Inspector David James of the Midlands police was waiting for them. The police officers shook hands before introducing the Inspector to Rachel and Catherine. He addressed the two women. "Can I say how very sorry I am for your loss? I can assure you that we will be as quick as we can. All I need you to do is identify the three people. You can do it simply by saying "Yes". They sat in Reception for five minutes until a technician came in.
"We are ready for you now."
They stood up quickly. Catherine grabbed Rachel's arm to steady her and didn't let go. They followed the technician into the viewing room. The room was carpeted in red. Paintings adorned all four walls and gentle piped music soothed its way out of four speakers hung in all four corners. Rachel saw and heard none of this. It took all her strength to take in the three shrouds lying on three trolleys laid out in a row.
Slowly and gently the technician drew back the shroud to reveal the top half of Andrew.
The sergeant and constable stood behind the sisters in case they needed support but they stood there in silence. Rachel whispered, "He had such a lovely chest." She bent over and kissed his forehead before nodding to the police

officers. The technician regathered the shroud before repeating the same actions for the two girls. Rachel kissed them both but did not cry. She couldn't. She couldn't cry because she couldn't believe it was happening. You can't cry over something that isn't happening.

They left the viewing room and re-entered the reception.

"Would you like a cup of tea?" asked the receptionist kindly.

"No thank you. I just want to get out of here."

The police officers shook hands with their colleague and within twenty minutes were speeding them back to her London home."

Sergeant Hay explained to them that the coroner would have to complete her report before the bodies could be released to an undertaker of her choice and that this would take about a week. The rest of the journey was completed in near total silence as Rachel lay in Catherine's embrace.

The Coroner's and Police reports indicated no foul play on the vehicle. From the lack of skid marks the report concluded that Andrew had fallen asleep. The car had collided with a petrol tanker, causing it to veer off the road before descending down the banking and ploughing into a hedge. The force of the impact at seventy miles an hour had killed all three occupants instantly.

Three months after the funeral, Rachel and her family were allowed to leave flowers and a wreath on the hedge.

The day was cold and black and driving rain showed them no kindness. The noise of traffic made conversation with family members almost impossible and filthy spray laced with petrol fumes added to the wetness of the rain. She could taste the fumes. The day was supposed to have been a commemoration. Instead, it was the worst of nightmares. Rachel turned to climb back to the car. She reached the top of the banking and thought to herself, "What a foul and disgusting world we have created."

The police car escorted them all back onto the motorway and safety. Andrew's brother drove Rachel and Catherine to Rachel's house. Eventually they arrived home. Her relatives fussed around her to no avail. She hardly noticed them. Catherine was the last to leave.

"Call me if you need me. It doesn't matter when. I will come."

Rachel nodded mechanically. Catherine turned her car round in the drive and the red lights disappeared onto the road. Rachel leant against the door frame absorbing the quiet. She could hear the silence in the house.

"What a foul and disgusting world."

CHAPTER 21

"You are a strong person and I know you'll get through this. I believe in you" were the last words of an email that Anne had just sent her. Twelve months had passed since her loss but the pain showed no sign of diminishing. The newspaper had been very supportive and Rachel had decided to throw herself into her career. She had been appointed as the newspaper's environment correspondent. It was a role which took her to meetings and events all over the world. She was enjoying her newfound status and the responsibility that came with it. It couldn't mask however, the emptiness she felt when she got home. Friends and relatives fussed around her and her success seemed to reassure them that all was as well as it could be. It was an illusion.

Her emails with Anne revealed a different picture. Both of them were dealing with their sense of loss and grief through their conversations with each other. These conversations were not ones of sympathy, although they did help one another through their dark moments, rather their discussions on environmental and political issues provided them with a never-ending stream of things to talk about and vent their anger upon.

At first Anne's were centred around hunting and Rachel's around pollution but over time they both seemed to be widening their subject matter and agreeing on most issues. They were rubbing off each other and developing a joint view on the world and its problems.

"When we were laying our wreaths by the roadside, the spray from the traffic hit me. It stunk of petrol fumes. I could taste petrol. I know you get angry about the hunting and so do I but it's more than that. Safari hunting is an extreme example of how we are damaging the earth but it's actually one small aspect amongst many and they are all linked."

"I couldn't agree more." Anne replied. "I'm not just angry about hunting. It's just one part of the whole. You can't just deal with one thing. It's the environment, world poverty and hunger set against excessive wealth. You can't preach against killing elephants for their tusks so long as there is a market for it and poor people need to feed their families."

Rachel, I am coming across to Edinburgh, Scotland next year. There's going to be a massive international United Nations Conference on climate change. There's going to be massive demonstrations and protests. Governments aren't doing enough and they need shaking to their boots. There are groups from America going and I've joined one of them. We could meet."

Rachel agreed immediately. Her diary was already full for that week as she had already been set to cover the conference. She could go, all expenses paid.

The next twelve months were busy ones for Rachel. She covered several so-called natural disasters over the whole world and even did a couple of reports live for BBC news. Her personal stock was rising but with each disaster she couldn't stop herself becoming even more depressed at the problems poor people faced. It was always the homes of poor people that were seen floating away down some raging African river. Of course, people in richer countries like America faced serious problems as well but they were fewer in number in comparison to the Third World. She was annoyed that the disasters in California seemed to get more coverage and yet they were commonplace elsewhere: so commonplace that they hardly constituted news anymore. People were living and dying in unnecessary misery. Amidst all this and her own personal grief, Rachel lived in a very heavy depression which she managed to barely control. Only her work and the sense that she was trying, in some small way, to improve the world kept her going.

In her emails to Anne she did not hide her feelings but Anne seemed less affected by David's death. She also seemed to have a strong sense of purpose towards creating change. She had a sense that change was possible if only you took action. She spoke about taking action several times in their correspondence but had not specified what that actually meant. Rachel was about to find out.

CHAPTER 22

The week of the International Conference duly arrived. They saw each other as often as they could that week. Rachel had access to the conference floor itself and was busy attending sessions in order to write articles on the progress or non-progress of the meetings. Anne attended several demonstrations. She had sat in on the alternative conference attended by activists from all over the world and had seen the potential of mass action when 100,000 people demonstrated outside the Conference centre on its last day. Anne had also seen the power of the state and its massed ranks of police dressed in riot gear and possessing tear gas, batons, dogs and horses that were arrayed against peaceful demonstrators. She didn't doubt for one minute that live ammunition was stored somewhere in those dozens of police vehicles that waited in the back streets.

They met each night, ate a meal together and discussed their day's experiences. At the beginning of the week both had been full of energy and enthusiasm. They had high hopes of the possibilities that the conference might bring. By the following Monday, their final day together, the enthusiasm had gone completely.

Anne and Rachel sat in a bar on Princes St looking up towards Castle Hill upon which stood the mighty 900 year old castle that dominated the entire scene. They had spent the entire afternoon getting drunk together. Both were in despair as streetlights began to brighten the darkening October sky but couldn't brighten their mood.

"It's all talk. It's all talk" Rachel fumed. "They'll sign treaties and agreements that have been watered down and then companies will simply find a way to get round the rules and regulations. The earth's doomed. We're all doomed."

Anne looked at her friend and nodded in silence.

"Another?" Rachel asked.

'Might as well."

Rachel returned with two large Chardonnays.

'I agree but for different reasons."

"What do you mean?'

"I knew the conference would be a whitewash. I never had faith in any politician but I did believe in the protests. I thought we could change things but not here, not this way. I saw people dressing up in costumes, singing songs of love and peace. How will dressing up like a Smurf change things? I mean, a bloody smurf! No one has really listened to us. Sure, we got on TV but we need more. We need direct action."

"What kind? What do you mean?"

Anne spoke quickly. "Some people are saying that we need a revolution but I don't know how that will happen.

All I know is what I can do, here, now, where I am."
Anne's mood changed suddenly as she continued to drink.
"Can I trust you?"
"Of course you can."
"I am going back to South Africa. I'm going to put that Safari out of business. These people are not listening. They need to be put out of action."
"How?"
"I'm going to shoot them."
"No. You can't."
"Who says?"
"It's murder. It's illegal."
"These big companies commit murder every day. They wipe people out, destroy villages and Governments help them. They are killers in suits and they get away with it."
After that they meet on a hunt and discuss international business whilst thoughtlessly killing animals. They don't give the animals a thought nor do they care for the lives of people they destroy. They are all the same people. The killing and the destruction of the environment. It's all the same people."
"But you can't kill people."
"Maybe I already have." she laughed.
Rachel's eyes were rolling in shock and horror at what she was thinking.
"Anne. Did you kill David?"

"Shhh!"

"Sorry." she whispered. "Anne, did you kill David?"

"Now I didn't say that did I?"

Rachel was trying to work out what Anne had just told her through a haze of alcohol.

She didn't, couldn't believe what she'd just heard and would she remember it in the morning?

It was time to leave. They were both drunk. Rachel would see her friend in the morning before she left for America. Their hotels were a mere hundred yards apart. As she embraced her friend Rachel hoped that by the morning the nightmare that seemed to be unfolding in Anne's head would turn out to be merely a dream.

CHAPTER 23

They said their goodbyes at the airport. There was a group of fellow protestors waiting to board the plane. Both were in good spirits.
"Look at them." Anne said dismissively. "They are all nice people who've spent a fortune to come here and protest in painted faces. They know nothing. It's so sad. That's why Governments always win; because they are up against "nice" people."
She looked at her friend. "If we are going to change the world we have got to change the protests. The time for pleasantries has gone. I can't do anything about the world but I can do something about hunting." She looked at Rachel earnestly. "I have a proposal for you. Think about what I've said. I'll contact you by phone in a week. I don't want to leave any trace of our conversations so don't mention them in your emails."
Rachel was bemused by what she was saying and the seriousness with which she said it. It seemed like she had descended into a spy movie. Half of her wanted to say "No I don't want anything to do with it," but the other half, more than half, was beguiled and intrigued. What was happening seemed so exciting. She was in another world, far away from the humdrum, survival mode that had been

her life since her family's death. It had an attraction that was too strong to resist despite her misgivings.

She stood there looking at her friend, lost in possibilities, when the announcement to board shook her out of her trance.

"OK." she nodded. "I'll wait to hear from you."

Anne turned to go and then turned back to face Rachel.

"I can trust you, can't I?" Rachel nodded.

"No matter what?"

"No matter what."

Rachel was surprised at herself as she watched Anne's plane taxi round onto the runway. She had no idea what Anne was proposing but suddenly Anne had given meaning to her meaningless existence and her heart soared as the plane disappeared into the Autumn sky.

CHAPTER 24

A week later Rachel received an envelope through the post. She opened it nervously. She knew it was from Anne. It contained one sheet of paper. On that single sheet was written a phone number and the words, "Buy a cheap phone and phone this number".

Rachel went to Tesco immediately and bought the cheapest phone available, took it home and put it on charge. The phone was ready to go.

She phoned the number.

"Hello?"

"Anne?"

"Yes? Rachel?"

They both laughed at the apparent ridiculousness of their behaviour.

"This is like something out of James Bond." Rachel laughed. Anne stopped her laughter in its tracks.

"Can I trust you?'

Rachel stopped smiling. "Of course you can. I told you so in Edinburgh."

"I killed David."

Rachel gasped.

"He beat me several times. I never told anyone. I know I should have done so but it's easier said than done. I felt no-one would believe me and then I'd have to go back to the house and face him. I hadn't got any money to live on my own. He controlled all the money we had through the business. I was so afraid."

"I understand".

Rachel said the words but they didn't quite ring true. She had had such a loving relationship with Andrew. She empathised would have been a better expression but she didn't understand how relationships could become so sour.

Anne was silent.

"Are you there?"

"Yes."

"Then he made me go on that awful safari. I've never hated anything so much in all my life. He told everyone it was a bonding exercise. Ha! He knew I'd hate it. He just wanted me to see him as he imagined his friends saw him; a hero, a mighty hunter. I despised him.

Then we came home and he insisted on mounting that poor animal's head on the wall in our front room.

I had to look at it every day. I was haunted by its eyes, looking at me and I found myself talking to it and apologising and then I thought why am I apologising? I am as much a victim as it was. One day he caught me talking to it. He laughed at me and that's when I decided to not only stop his violence to me but to his other victims as well. I decided their lives were more valuable, more worthwhile than his because he had a choice to behave like he did. They didn't.

I decided to kill him. Not to kill him, to dispatch him. That's the word they use when the animal is lying there helpless and dying. I dispatched him."

The silence was profound.

"I understand."

This time Rachel actually did. Anne had put into words all the confused thoughts she had experienced since her time on the safari and her anger at the loss of her cherished husband and children. She had come to realise that human life was brief and ultimately as futile as those animals in the jungle. Life is born, it lives and it dies and that's all there is to it.

"How do you feel about going back to South Africa?" Anne asked.

"To do what?"

"To begin the end of the killing."

"You mean kill those on the safari?"

"I wouldn't put it like that. I'd rather say to begin, 'a war on terror,' the terror of hunting."

"Is that not playing with words?"

"It's only doing what they do. In fact, when you think about it, those words are a damn site nearer to the truth than those used by politicians in places like Iraq."

Rachel hesitated.

"I'll come with you but I can't be involved in murder. I just want to be near you."

Rachel wasn't sure why she had said yes to Anne's invitation or what she expected to be doing. Somewhere in her head she probably thought that she could stop her friend from getting into trouble whilst she killed people and then there was the not too simple matter of Anne's confession to killing her husband. What was she supposed to do? If she didn't tell the police about what she knew then it involved her in the crime.

Rachel realised that she was not thinking clearly but her overwhelming concern was simply to be near her friend at a critical and dangerous moment in her life. She needed support. It was as simple as that.

CHAPTER 25

In mid-March they boarded a plane bound for South Africa. Anne had made all the arrangements. They were spending a fortnight at the same ranch as before. She had explained to Zach that she wanted to visit the place where David had had his happiest moment as a hunter and that it would help her to bring closure to his murder.

Zach had been horrified and very supportive and had done everything in his power to make the arrangements as quick and simple as he could.

Zach understood the trauma she must have been going through. He had received similar death threats in recent months and it was obvious his business and the whole activity of hunting was being threatened by some organised group. The South African police had taken the threats seriously and had interviewed the small number of known activists but had few clues to go on. What was particularly worrying was that the death threats had been sent by post, thereby letting the police know that the threat was local and therefore real. When Zach learnt of David's murder in America he contacted Captain Stransky at Polokwane police to see if they had spoken to the American police. To his relief they had but the American police had not been able to offer much help. Lieutenant

McLellan had sent him a file on the case which offered little to go on. What was interesting was that the only possible suspect had remained the wife of one of the ranch's previous customers Anne Mulhern. This was duly noted but again there was no evidence to go on and Zach dismissed the thought s preposterous.

Meanwhile the police continued to run extra helicopter flights over the ranch and outlying areas but there was little they could do. The area covered several hundred square miles. Spotting a possible suspicious vehicle was virtually impossible and they had enough problems of a routine nature to deal with. Each incident involved a huge commitment of resources. They were also facing increased demands as a result of poaching. They simply couldn't provide the cover.

At least the ranch had armed personnel on regular duty. Its activities provided a regular security system but it didn't mean it was invulnerable. The plain fact was that they would have to look after themselves.

Zach's safari activities also had problems with criminal gangs of poachers coming onto his land in order to take elephant tusks and rhino horns. He didn't want his customers to discover the bloated carcasses of mutilated elephants. It simply wasn't a good look for his business. They were also facing another problem. Someone had been interfering with the fencing separating his estate from the Kruger National Park. Whoever it was knew what they were doing. The fencing had been cut down near known lion territories and these animals had strayed onto his land. So far, the small number of incidents had been dealt with fairly quickly but they were an unnecessary distraction.

Despite all these problems his business was doing very well and he looked forward to welcoming Anne and the woman who had written the article about his ranch. He hadn't particularly enjoyed reading it but there was no doubt that whilst it had cast hunting in a bad light it had seemed to have the effect of advertising his business. The story hadn't harmed his business as he had feared it might although it had been helped by the fact that 2 rival safari organisations had closed down recently.

One thing that perplexed him though was what were these women who were not going to be hunting going to do? He was about to find out.

CHAPTER 26

Johnathan was waiting for them at the airport.
He recognised them immediately. Anne went straight to him and put her arms around him. Rachel was obviously surprised and Anne laughed.
"We have been keeping in touch on a regular basis," she explained. "He knows everything," she whispered. "He's on our side."
Suddenly Rachel realised that something was going on that was much bigger than she had imagined. Perhaps Anne didn't need help at all. Perhaps she had been naive. If she had been, it meant that she had questions to ask and required answers. Who else was involved? What was Anne actually planning? What would Rachel have to do? Would she be happy being involved? Could she get out of it now and more importantly, did she want to get out?
"Come on. It's going to be OK. Honest."
They climbed in the Ranger vehicle as Johnathan loaded their luggage.
Within minutes they were on the highway heading towards the ranch. Eventually they turned off the highway and began the 7-mile trek that led to the perimeter of the ranch.
"Pull over there."

Jonathan brought the vehicle to a halt and Anne turned to Rachel.

"Right, I need to tell you what's going on. Jonathan and I have been in touch on a regular basis by letter. No emails, no phone calls, no trace. Letters have been destroyed after being read. We are deadly serious. We are going to stop hunting safaris by direct action. Already our members have been sabotaging fencing in farms which breed wild animals for killing. If you set a group of lions free it causes all kinds of problems for owners and police. They can't guarantee the safety of their operations. We've really upset their businesses and two ranches have terminated their operations in the last year. They haven't made any official announcements because they don't want to put clients off by letting them know it may not be safe. The authorities are really worried and we are going to keep up and increase the disruption. This business is not acceptable. We all have our reasons why but we are united in the need to stop this. Aren't we?"

She looked at Johnathan.

"Yes. I've had enough. They are destroying tribal life, our culture. They try to show that they are the good guys by bringing us meat. It is our meat. We have hunted for centuries. We don't want their so-called help. We can fend for ourselves."

"How many people are involved?"

"Just a few. It's not big. We don't want to be. The more people, the easier it is for something to go wrong. We've got them really worried but we need just one big statement to show they have to stop. They can mend fences and catch the lions. What we have done so far creates an inconvenience but we now need to do something that will make them question their own commitment to what they are doing."

"What do you want me to do?"

"Nothing!"

Rachel looked shocked.

"Well not exactly nothing." Anne laughed.

I want you to provide a diversion to help confuse the police's investigation.

You are not here for the hunting so they'll want to know what you're doing here and whether you were involved in any of the shootings.

"Oh OK." Rachel said uncertainly.

Rachel now realised that Anne was perfectly serious in everything she was about to do. She had come along with her in some vague hope that she could stop her friend from getting involved in some fanciful scheme. She had hoped that maybe she could protect her friend who had suffered the trauma of losing her husband. She had thought that somehow the shared experience of their husbands' deaths might help to bring Anne to her senses.

Now, she understood that her friend did not need anyone's protection. She saw that Anne had a clearly worked out position and direction. It was Rachel who was confused. She was angry with the hunters and their activities. She desperately wanted to stop them. She also had not come to terms with the deaths of her husband and daughters. It wasn't Anne who needed help and guidance it was Rachel. She wanted to stop the killings but she was unsure about how far she wanted to go. Anne would argue that she couldn't stop the killings by wanting them to stop. She had to take action to make them stop. Maybe Anne was right.

They arrived at the ranch about 3.00pm and settled into their rooms.

At about 5.00pm Zach called on them to discuss their activities during the stay. Much of the detail had been discussed online but Zach felt the need to finalise things in person.

It was agreed that the women would attend two hunts. Rachel spun a story about taking videos for a tv documentary she was involved in. Rachel also intended to go to a photographic safari to see an alternative type of safari and Zach suggested they have a look at the farm area where they had started raising wild animals for release into the wild in order for the animals to be hunted.

In the meantime, they enjoyed their evening meal and were introduced to the rest of the hunting party. Two brothers, Michael and Guy, from New England looked like the most unlikely of hunters. They were short, thin and balding and both wore spectacles with thick lenses. Rachel wondered if they would be able to see a target, let alone hit one. They looked almost ridiculous carrying their large hunting rifles which fired 577 Nitro Express bullets that were powerful enough to down a Cape buffalo with one shot.

She also met Karl and Madeleine from New York and talked with them for some time. They were married and owned a dental practice and in Madeleine's words "got out of the city as often as possible."

Rachel was particularly interested in Madeleine. She was 36 years old. At 5 foot 7 inches she was very athletic and well-muscled. She obviously worked out on a regular basis and enjoyed hunting. Unlike Anne, she was definitely not the timid wife of a hunting husband. Rachel felt that there might be some sort of story possible here regarding women who get involved in hunting but that would have to wait for now. Manuel, a Mexican, seemed a different proposition altogether. He was in his early forties, tanned with jet black hair. He stood at 6 foot, was heavy chested and looked like he could wrestle a bear. They were a strange group who talked about nothing else but their hunting exploits. Apparently the two brothers belied their physical appearance and had hunted all over the world. They described their occupations as "in finance" and had obviously been very successful, seeming to spend a fortune on their hobby.

Manuel was very reserved and said very little. Rachel felt there was a menace about him but she couldn't define it. He just spent the evening watching them all.

"Maybe he's just shy," said Anne. "I didn't sense anything untoward." Rachel was not convinced. His whole demeanour appeared to offer a threat. Did he know something? Was he on to them? Was he a police spy? Rachel was excited and yet frightened and she didn't trust the Mexican.

CHAPTER 27

After their meal Anne and Rachel spent time in the courtyard, warmed by the fire pit. It reminded her of the evening she had spent with Kyle nearly two years earlier. She smiled at the strange feelings he had aroused in her although nothing had happened between them.
"Do you remember Kyle?" Rachel asked.
"Yes. Why?"
"I was wondering that's all. I haven't seen him." Just then Johnathan appeared carrying some bags to one of the vehicles. He turned to the women.
"I'm sorry ladies but Kyle is dead."
"What? No! How?"
Johnathan put the bags in the vehicle and came over to them.
"Shall I sit?"
"Of course."
He pulled one of the metal chairs and sat in front of the two women. He rested his forearms on his thighs and clasped his hands together before looking at them both in the eyes.
"As far as we know he was in Namibia with a Government agency dealing with tusk and horn hunters. About 9 months ago they caught a group who were removing tusks

from a dead elephant. At dusk they went to arrest them and there was a firefight. Two of the hunters were killed and three arrested. Kyle was shot and was thought to have fallen into a ravine. By the time the fighting was over it was dark. They searched for Kyle for over an hour before it became impossible to continue. When they returned in the morning all they found in the ravine was his rifle, a boot and parts of his uniform. The official version of his death was that he had fallen into the ravine as a result of being shot and was taken in the night, probably by a lion."
"You said 'official version' do you think there is another explanation?"
"Who is to say? He was working for a Government agency against criminal gangs. Some people in the villages believe he has disappeared for some reason but maybe it's just talk.
"What do you think?" asked Rachel, desperate to believe that he was still alive.
"The fact is no one knows. He didn't plan to disappear. He was shot in a gunfight with criminals. People have all kinds of theories but nobody knows. The fact is Kyle is no longer with us."
Jonathan rose from his seat. "I liked Kyle. He was a good man. You know his parents were murdered?"
The women nodded. "Yes, he told me." said Rachel.

"He always seemed sad to me. Even when he was laughing. Anyway, I go to bed now. See you in the morning."

"Goodnight."

The two women remained in silence. Rachel was thinking about the evening she had spent sitting in the very spot she was sitting in now, lost in her fantasy.

"I need another drink."

"Get me one please."

"Large?"

"Absolutely"

Rachel brought them back from the bar. They drank quickly and in silence. They were stunned. Anne got up and took Rachel's glass without asking. She did not protest.

"The world's a fucking awful mess," thought Rachel. "You can't even have a sexual fantasy without it being ruined by reality." She thought of him being dragged away to be eaten and hoped that the stories in the villages were true.

Anne returned a moment later. They drank that glass quickly as well.

"I think it's time for bed." Anne said.

Rachel sighed. "Yep, I suppose you're right."

They got up together, placed their empty glasses on the counter and went to their rooms. Both were asleep within minutes and if she dreamt, Rachel did not remember it.

CHAPTER 28

Just as she did on her previous visit, Rachel woke up to the sound of gun fire. This time she knew it meant people were fine tuning their weapons to ensure maximum accuracy.

Anne was still asleep and snoring heavily but had woken up by the time Rachel had finished showering.

"I woke up and my first thought was of Kyle."

Rachel was surprised by this. She wasn't aware that Anne had had any contact with Kyle.

"Ah well. Shit happens," she replied. There was nothing else she could say.

"I suppose you are right."

They ate a full breakfast before meeting Zach at 9.00am. He was going to take them on a tour of the new facilities at the ranch.

"Good morning ladies, are you ready?".

While the rest of the party prepared their weapons and reconnoitred the terrain of the ranch, Zach took the two friends on a tour of the wildlife farm he had created since their previous visit.

"It was a neighbouring farm until two years ago. The owner died and I bought the property. It's bigger than my ranch, nearly 70 square miles. He used to grow oranges.

We've turned all that over to wildlife farming. We are adding to the populations, not taking them away." He gave a knowing look towards Rachel who simply smiled back without speaking.

It was Anne who asked the next question.

"So let me get this right. You operate as a farm rearing a variety of species. How many are reared and how many are killed?"

"About 80% are killed."

He looked straight into the camera that Rachel was holding.

"Look no animal in the wild dies of old age. They are all eaten in the end. They get injured and can't keep up. Eventually a predator will pick them off; we are just maintaining the supply and actually increasing it. You need to write something about those tusk hunters. Now they are the real threats to elephants and rhinos. We have turned land over to wildlife.

They toured the sheds where many animals were housed. In one shed thick tubular steel fencing held one male and one female white rhinoceros. To Rachel's untrained eye the space allocated seemed more than adequate and there was access to land outside. It looked like a European zoo.

"You don't hunt these do you. Aren't they endangered?" she asked.

Yes they are and no, we don't hunt them. This compound is part of a Government initiative to re-populate the rhino. This female is pregnant and we hope to produce many more over her lifetime."

"Will they be shot?"

"They will be released into the wild by Government agents as they mature. What happens after their release is not under our control although our staff do cooperate with Government anti-poaching agencies to try and prevent poachers."

"But not hunters?'

Zach sighed wearily. "I don't have a crystal ball."

Other compounds contained a variety of animals. The range was quite impressive and the cleanliness seemed to her untutored eye to be exemplary.

"How does this kind of hunting work?"

"The animals are released into fenced-off areas. We know where they are so we go and look for them. It's much easier and cheaper for the hunters. We've seen a big increase in the number of hunters. It's not just a rich man's thing anymore."

"You said it as if that were a good thing. Doesn't that mean more animals are killed?"

"And more are bred," he interrupted.

"Come!" he commanded, "We go and see the lion compound."

They drove several hundred yards to the lions. Jonathan and a farm labourer were standing in the rear of a truck throwing meat over the high red metal fence.

Rachel counted 7 lions. She had to admit they looked in good condition and were eager for the food that was landing at their feet.

"What do you feed them?"

"We try to vary it as much as we can. We get chickens from a neighbouring chicken farm, meat from an abattoir. Some of the meat caught on hunts is also used."

"What is the meat they are feeding them now?"

"Er they are stillborn calves from the abattoir. Nothing is wasted."

Rachel nodded. "I understand. You are paying respect to the animals by not wasting it?"

"Exactly. As I said, we waste nothing."

They stood there in silence as the lions devoured their "prey".

After a few minutes Zach said, "I have to go now. Johnathan will look after you for the rest of the tour."

Rachel thanked him for his time. Zach half smiled; half grunted. She wasn't certain whether he was pleased with her interest or resented it. As she watched him drive off, she turned and saw Anne and Johnathan in conversation together. They were standing by the fence and she filmed them for a moment as a lion stood near them, watching them.

"Oh hi. Jonathan was just telling me that he is taking us to a water hole."

For some strange reason Rachel did not believe her. "What else would they be talking about?" she reasoned but it still didn't feel right. For a moment she watched the lion watching them.

"How does it view us?"

"As food," replied Johnathan, nothing else. It's not personal."

Rachel smiled. The animal seemed so peaceful as it issued a quiet growling noise but she understood the menace it represented. "Not nice outside your village," she thought.

The vehicle that had brought meat to the cats had now departed and Rachel realised that they were the only visible source of meat available to them. She was only too willing to enter Johnathan's Ranger when he called them both to get in.

"Where are we going now?"

"I will take you to the water hole. We can see some animals there."

They approached a huge gate that resembled the ones she had seen in the Jurassic Park films.

Johnathan pressed a button on the gate's frame and it slowly opened before clanking against the fence. He drove through a short distance towards a second gate by which time the first gate had slammed into its frame. He then repeated the procedure.

They travelled for approximately fifteen minutes before Johnathan brought the Ranger to a halt under the shade of a huge Baobab tree. Rachel looked around her. She could see no sign of a water hole.

"It's a short walk but we don't want the vehicle to make the animals wary."

Rachel and Anne got out. They walked for a couple of minutes before arriving at a small clearing in the middle of which sat a small water hole.

About fifteen yards to one side of the hole stood an animal hide. It resembled an American Indian teepee. About twelve feet tall and covered in some kind of fabric it was camouflaged by a covering of branches and leaves. They entered and sat on a bench which gave all three of them a view of the water hole. Instinctively they spoke in whispers. A couple of deer came down for a drink.

"Is this what your clients do? They sit here and wait for an animal to come to drink and then shoot it?"

"That's about it," nodded Johnathan. "It's very simple."

"It's too easy. It doesn't seem like hunting."

"The water hole is man made. It is piped in and yes it makes it all very simple and easy. Anyone can come and hunt. It's much cheaper than the usual hunting and you don't need much skill. The number of animals being killed has soared. It's ten times what it was. More."

Suddenly the animals disappeared and it became very quiet. Then, suddenly a lion came into view across the other side of the hole. Johnathan quickly and silently closed the viewing flap which put them in semi darkness.
"That's very strange. This is a fenced off site. A lion shouldn't be here."
"What do we do?"
"Stay still and quiet. I have a gun in the Ranger but it's too far away".
The lion stopped to drink. They watched it slowly edge its way round the water hole as it headed towards them. Within seconds they could hear it panting outside. It moved slowly towards the front of the hide. It pawed the fabric which resisted well. Just then a vehicle sped to a halt near to the frightened occupants and the lion ran off.
Footsteps came round and Johnathan opened the door.
"Am I glad to see you," said Anne.
Zach nodded. "Bring your Ranger here and take them back."
'You should have had your gun with you."
"I know. I'm sorry. I never thought that we would encounter a lion here."
"Someone has cut a hole in the perimeter fence."

"What?"

"We are under attack my friend. Keep your gun with you at all times."

Zach rode off with two members of staff. It took them three hours to catch the lion and dart it before returning it to the compound. They then had to repair the fence.

He sat in his office with a glass of whisky in his hand. This was bad, very bad. Someone had got to his caged lions. Were they the same people who had, over the last couple of years, been issuing death threats to him? He had got used to them and had treated them as idle threats. This was now evidence that they were serious and getting organised. They were his enemy but he had no idea of who they were. Then a strange thought occurred to him. "Could those women somehow be involved? They had nothing to do with the hunts. Were they up to something?"

He laughed at his stupidity. They were two middle class widows from Europe and North America. How could they possibly be involved?" He poured another drink. He was letting the situation get to him and he had no time for ridiculous fears to spook him. He had a hunt to organise for the next day.

Rachel and Anne spent the evening in their room talking in whispers. They had been frightened and exhilarated by the events of the afternoon.

"What's happening Anne?"

Anne turned to her and smiled serenely. "Soon," she said, "Very soon."

CHAPTER 29

The next morning Anne came to Rachel's room before breakfast.
"I need to speak to you. The plans are almost in place."
"What plans Anne? I need to know what I am getting involved in."
This morning we are going on a hunt. I've spoken to Zach. We need to create the illusion that we are part of his activities. I want him to believe that not only am I in mourning for David but I'm also into hunting. I don't want us to appear too different from the others. You need to bring your camera and do some videos. If the police become interested in why you are here we need to make certain that you can show them that you have been doing work as you said you would and I need to look like I am getting involved in the hunt as I said I wanted to be."
"When?"
"When what?"
"When are you going to do," she paused, "it".
"Friday."
Today is Wednesday. Why Friday?"
Tomorrow you are going on that safari hunt."
"Listen Anne, I came to be with you and support you. I haven't said I wanted to go further."

"You will do, after today and tomorrow."
"Look, I know that today I'm going on a hunt and it will be awful but I've seen it before I know what to expect. I know that this is an awful place but today's hunt isn't going to turn me into a terrorist or a freedom fighter."
"But you are already here. You are halfway. Think about it. Before all the awful things that have happened would you have seen yourself coming back here?"
"No."
"You're here because you are angry and want things to change but you don't know how. What we do know is that you are here and not at home tutting over a cup of tea. You are reaching out but are frightened. That's OK. I won't ask you to do anything you don't want to."
Anne moved to the door. "In the end it's your choice." She smiled. "See you outside."
Rachel sighed. She was confused and uncertain, paralysed by fear. Yes, that was it, the plain fact was that she was frightened.
She collected her things and went outside to the Ranger. A moment later Anne came out carrying a rifle over her shoulder. Rachel couldn't believe her eyes. For a few minutes they were alone in the vehicle.
"Why are you carrying that?"
"To put people off guard. I asked Zach if I could hire a rifle and join the hunt. There'll be no suspicion on me."

The party set out at 6.00 am. Zach sat in the front with Johnathan by his side. They drove for nearly two hours to an area that Rachel and Anne did not recognise. They stopped by a river that was flowing slowly into more lush vegetation. Already Rachel could feel a tension rising in her. The terrain wasn't exactly deep jungle but it was definitely an area in which animals could hide. Zach spoke quietly. He sent Johnathan twenty yards ahead and to the left with the four hunters.

"Keep close to me and don't speak." he whispered to the two women.

They had been tracking for over 2 hours and the heat was rising rapidly as the sun moved overhead. The shade of the trees did little to assuage its effects. They stopped for a brief drink of water as shirts darkened with sweat. They had to make a kill soon or abort the hunt. Zach was concerned that the heat and terrain would exhaust his clients. He put his water bottle to his mouth and froze in disbelief. Standing no more than fifty yards away was a huge male lion.

He motioned to everyone to keep low.

"What the fuck!" whispered Zach. "Stay here and don't move!"

Without warning Madeleine stood up and shot at the lion and appeared to hit it in the rear. It spun round one hundred and eighty degrees before disappearing into increasingly dense vegetation which would provide cover for the lion and danger to the humans. Zach could not believe what she had just done. It was either an act of blind panic or a desire not to miss this opportunity that made her incapable of following the expedition leader's instructions.

This was now a very serious situation. Unless he was fatally damaged the lion posed a real threat to his clients. On the other hand, if they withdrew and the lion survived, even temporarily, it would pose a real threat to others until a hunting party of professionals could be brought in to dispatch it. There was a silent chaos as Zach pulled everyone together and whispered terse instructions.

"Listen everyone. We need to follow him and finish this quickly for our safety and to eliminate his pain. We have to be quick but not stupid. Spread out a little.

They followed a trail of blood down to a stream that ran through a gully carved out of sandstone rock. The lion was obviously losing a lot of blood. Then the trail seemed to disappear. Without warning Manuel dashed forward in excitement. He ran through the stream and jumped onto a large rock.

"It's here. It's dead!"

Zach screamed, "Get back!" Manuel turned to the others when the lion sprung at him.

He let out a terrifying and prolonged scream as he fell under the weight of the huge cat whose teeth sank into him. A volley of shots rang out. All missed and hit surrounding rocks. The snarling lion let out a strange scream and turned to make one last dash for freedom. Zach took aim when two shots rang out to his right and stopped the animal in its tracks. It fell dead. Zach and Rachel turned in amazement. Both their mouths hung open as they gazed on the erect figure of Anne, still holding her pose as if awaiting a photograph.

Zach dashed forward and Rachel was surprised at his speed and agility. He was obviously a man who had experienced the danger of conflict and knew how to handle himself despite his middle-aged bulk. As he moved away from them towards the lion Rachel turned to her friend.

"What? Where did that come from?'

"I put the poor creature out of his misery. What else could I do?"

"But where, when did you learn to shoot like that?"

"It's a secret. Anyway it will give me some kudos with the others. They won't expect anything from me."

'Why? What?" Rachel sat there, looking at her friend with a mixture of awe and disbelief.

"Come on my friend. We need to help with that wounded human."

In the maelstrom of emotions and events that surrounded her Rachel had completely forgotten about him. As she moved towards him she saw the lifeless body of the lion and turned towards the shaking bloodied form of Manuel who let out a sort of miaow like an injured domestic cat. Zach had checked that the lion was dead and he and his staff moved its body to allow access to Manuel who was showing clear signs of shock. Rachel moved to calm him as best she could. In an earlier existence, before becoming a journalist, she had served as a nurse and later a midwife. With the arrival of her children, she had decided to train as a journalist and had worked part-time as a freelancer. It allowed her to work around her children's needs and it was work she enjoyed much more than nursing.

Zach joined her and brought a large and comprehensive first-aid pack from the Ranger.

He was obviously experienced at treating wounds. Rachel wondered whether he had gained this experience as a soldier or from previous encounters with wild animals. "I was a nurse," she shouted to a question that hadn't been asked.

"Army medical-corp," replied Zach. The two of them worked in tandem, quickly and efficiently. They ripped off his tattered sleeve and revealed three six inch claw marks down his forearm. They also saw a puncture mark from a tooth, just above his bicep. His shirt was covered in blood from wounds which were deep and bleeding profusely but, luckily, there was no sign of a pulsing blood flow, suggesting that no arteries had been ruptured. They applied pads and bound them tightly. Jonathan took a saline drip out of a large cooler bag and inserted a cannula in Manuel's free arm. The whole operation was completed within minutes.

"How many drips do you have?" asked Rachel.

"One more in the chiller bag." They last about a half hour each.

They sat him up and kept his arm elevated before loading him into the back of the vehicle and sat him with his back against the rear window of the cabin.

Zach had arranged for an air ambulance helicopter to meet them at a nearby waterhole which was readily identifiable on the map. It would take approximately 15 minutes to get there. Manuel had now calmed down and then amazingly he asked for the lion to be loaded alongside him. Rachel watched in disbelief as the injured man began talking to the deceased animal.

"What a noble animal." He stroked its mane.

"What a fine adversary." He patted it.

He shouted to Zach "Can I have him? I want to look at him and be reminded of how I survived."

Zach nodded. "We charge a fee."

"Of course. It's worth every peso."

"I shall mount him in my front room."
At one point Manuel leant over and kissed the lion.
Rachel was horrified and baffled. It wasn't as if he had even killed the poor thing. Anne and Zach had. Everyone stood in silence, mesmerised by the whole scene.
'We have to go," roared Zach. "Come on, let's move!"
Rachel followed behind in the Ranger as the truck made slow and gentle progress to the water hole. The journey took twenty minutes. They parked the vehicles in clear sight and the helicopter landed within minutes. As they prepared to load him on board and separate him from his prize, Manuel asked Zach to take a photograph of him alongside his victim. Moments later he was airborne. The party of professional hunters and clients stood motionless and silent looking after the helicopter long after it had disappeared from view.
"Well. That's a relief. Let's hope he recovers quickly," said Zach.
Rachel looked at Zach who was standing with his hands resting on the truck.
 "I thought you said there weren't any lions roaming free."
Zach spoke into the distant horizon. "There aren't or rather there shouldn't be." His face bore a pained look. "That's the second in a matter of days. This is bad. This is very bad. This has never happened before." He paused, turned to face her and spoke slowly.' If I didn't know any better.

I'd say that someone is trying to ruin me." He paused for a while and then said, "Bye the way. You did really well."
"Thank you. So did you. So did everyone. Your staff are well trained."
"It's all part of customer service." he smiled "for as long as we last anyway."
No one spoke on the way back.
There was nothing left to say.

CHAPTER 30

To everyone's amazement, Manuel returned to the ranch two days later. He entered the dining room, just before the evening meal was about to commence, smiling from ear to ear. He received applause from his fellow hunters as if he were a champion prize-fighter returning home to his village but he was not in champion condition.
"I had two pints of blood and forty stitches in three wounds, then today I discharged myself. I'm good but weak and I can't fly home for a week. Well, I wasn't going to anyway." Everyone joined in the laughter but it was obvious he was weakened and would be taking no further part in the activities of the ranch.
They sat down to eat. Manuel managed a bowl of soup before retiring for the night.
Despite his ordeal he was proud of his achievement and his survival. He would return home knowing that the head of the "lion that nearly got me," would be mounted on his lounge wall.
This struck Rachel as very strange. Manuel had done nothing but get caught by the animal and savaged. He had wriggled on the floor in helpless agony as its teeth sank into him. Yet the event had given him an almost legendary status from his colleagues.

She was glad that he would be returning home to his wife and children. No one wanted to see him dead but how could being a victim make you more of a man? His wanting to pat the lion's body in the wagon had seemed strange. Now this seemed to border on insanity. It was a world she didn't understand or want. The whole attitude to animals seemed insane and cruel and she wanted it stopped. She was getting angrier with every event she witnessed but she still had one hope of an alternative left.

Tomorrow she was going on a day out with a photographic safari group. This held out a hope of a better alternative to hunting. A hope that somehow the animals of Africa could be seen in a different light. A hope that perhaps humankind could view animals as fellow beings on this earth rather than seeing them as their playthings. She couldn't wait.

CHAPTER 31

The next morning Rachel left the ranch at 6.00am. Jonathan drove her the thirty miles to the Johannesfontein safari reserve situated in the Kruger National park. She entered the visitor centre and was greeted by a beautiful young woman dressed in bush clothing.
"Hello. My name is Kaya. I will be your guide today.
Rachel was struck immediately by the difference between the two types of safari organisations. Here there were far more people in attendance and the gender balance was quite different being almost equally male and female. Many of the clients were obviously couples.
The only equipment on view were cameras and extending lenses, tripods and equipment covers. People were busying themselves checking battery levels and lenses between sips of coffee and chats to their neighbours.
A young woman came into the room and began shaking hands with people. She was blonde and petite and gently spoken with a beaming smile that immediately made the room feel smaller and warm. After a few minutes chatting she introduced herself formally to the group as the leader of the morning activity.
"Hello, I'm Emily Davidson and this is Robert, my assistant. The contrast between the two was stark. At 6-ft 2

inches he stood over her. His skin colour indicated that he had spent many hours outside in the bush whilst hers suggested that she spent considerable effort in protecting her skin. Despite her small stature and pale skin she was quite clearly the one in command.

"First of all, I would like to welcome you to Safari Photographs Johannesfontein and thank you for booking with us. The name of our reserve refers to a marshy wet area belonging to Johannes and its main focus lies at a water hole where you will be able to see several species of animals who come to the hole. It is fed by an underground spring and has never dried up. You will be able to see; elephants, cape buffalo, zebras, antelope and the occasional lion. There are also a wide variety of birds.
We have been in existence now for 5 years and set up this company deliberately to establish a respect for wildlife and create a celebration of South Africa. We want to photograph it and enjoy it, not kill it."
With that the small audience broke into applause. Emily smiled.
"We hope you will enjoy today. South Africa is a beautiful country. The scenery is awe-inspiring and the range of wildlife is wonderful. Of course, like any expedition, we cannot guarantee that you will see everything you want to see. If you pardon the expression, we do have to hunt the

game; it doesn't present itself voluntarily for a photoshoot." She smiled and again the audience laughed.
Rachel warmed to her immediately and couldn't help thinking of the distinct contrast between this and the hunting group. There was excitement in the air instead of tension and she warmed to the people immediately. Emily continued. "We shall be getting into our vehicles in a moment and our drivers and guides will introduce themselves to you. Can I remind you, and you will find that this occurs several times, that you are on a safari. The animals are wild and we are entering their domain. At all times you must respect these animals and the dangers they represent. Please listen to your guides who are only acting in your interests and do not take any liberties that might provoke the anger of the animals."
She paused for a minute to let her message sink in, smiled and concluded her talk by saying, "And on that note I hope you have a lovely day and find the expedition most rewarding."
With that she opened the door to the outside and escorted the congregation out to the waiting vehicles. There was a clear excitement and anticipation for the day ahead.

Rachel climbed up into an extended Land Rover vehicle with a covered roof and unnervingly open sides. The guide was already seated in the vehicle. He waited until everyone was seated and had sorted their belongings out.

"Hello. My name is Nelson and I am your guide and driver. Don't worry the sides are open to allow you to take clear photographs."

"Don't the animals try to get in?" asked Rachel.

Nelson smiled "No they're not really interested in us. We are far more interested in them. They're more concerned with their everyday business than boring photographers."

Rachel sat down and realised that she was the only one without a high-quality camera.

"Are you not taking any photographs?" said a woman with an obvious American accent. She was tall, slim and tanned with auburn hair and huge sunglasses.

"Hi I'm Lucy." she beamed. "Is this your first Safari?"

"Well, I'm a reporter," replied Rachel "and I'm doing a report for an English newspaper about hunting safaris and I thought that I'd spend a day with a photographic safari to do a comparison, you know, to compare the activities and the types of people and to do stories about them."

"Oh, how interesting." and without invitation she launched into an account of her life. Rachel was able to discover that Lucy was 49 years old, divorced and was determined to enjoy life.

"I got a really good settlement out of the divorce from Gerry. He was a bank manager in Ohio and we were very comfortable until one day I discovered him in bed, I mean our bed with his secretary! I kicked him out and now I'm here enjoying myself, the swine!"

Rachel smiled. She hadn't intended to do a comparative account. It was a little white lie but she reflected on the fact that maybe she had stumbled on an idea for the future. She took notes and a photograph on her phone. She always took notes; it was never possible to forecast when they might come in handy. She had become so embroiled in this conversation that she had not noticed that the vehicle was now moving across rough terrain and due to its lack of rigid sides was leading them on a very bumpy ride. Rachel grabbed one of the uprights and then made a mental note not to do that when they were near any animals.

"I can't bear the thought of going on one of those hunting safaris. I mean how cruel and why? Why do you need to kill the animal? Why not just enjoy them? There's no call for it. It just seems to me that they are mostly a bunch of ageing men with big guns and little dicks! Mmm, maybe if Jerry had gone on a hunt he might not have put his dick in his secretary!" She laughed. "Mind you his dick wasn't that small! she burst into raucous laughter and immediately began to cough. "The swine!"

Apart from the bouncing around the journey was very similar to that of a hunting safari

'Ssshhh!" Nelson the guide brought the Rover to an immediate halt. In the distance they could see a small group of animals that she recognised but couldn't remember the name of. "Gnu, Wildebeest," whispered Nelson. There's about 15 of them who seem to have moved away from the rest of the herd".

The vehicles slowed and dipped round a bend. Rachel was surprised as a group of 6 more vehicles came into view. They had a different logo on the doors and were obviously from another safari group. She could see cameras poised at the ready. Altogether they formed a group of 9 vehicles standing at the top of the slope as if they were grazing animals. Rachel watched as photographers pushed forward in order to get the best shot. The noise of clicking cameras was almost deafening and rapid. "Lion!" Nelson hissed. Softly, urgently, cameras whirled round and began to focus on this developing scene. A husband demanded of his wife that she produce the video camera from its bag.

"There's going to be some real action here," he said. "We need to get it on film." Immediately she dragged a case from beneath her seat and produced the biggest video camera Rachel had ever seen. As she began to film, the lion made its move and chased one of the wildebeest across the banking which stood in front of the vehicles. In a panic the snorting animal turned into the cluster of vehicles. Finding its path blocked it turned to face its assailant who had been joined by a second lioness. The wildebeest attempted to gore the first with its twin horns but to no avail. The big cat overpowered it immediately, grabbing at its throat in order to suffocate it by squeezing its windpipe. Cameras clicked rapidly as people tried to get the best view of the "action".

The momentum of the collision between two large animals saw them slam into the side of the vehicle with enormous force and the vehicle shook under the pressure.

Rachel recoiled as the victim screamed in fear. It was horrifying. She had no problem with the lion killing for its food; that was nature in all its brutal glory. Rachel objected to the people on the safari enjoying themselves whilst trying to get a good photograph of the kill. They claimed to be more in touch with nature than those who shot animals yet here they were, so engrossed that they had no thought for an animal's suffering.

The vehicles remained stationary and turned the engines off whilst this event unfolded. Eventually the wildebeest succumbed and the lion dragged its victim away in order to consume it. As it disappeared into the trees the engines fired up and moved on to the next sighting.

"Wow, wasn't that amazing?" said Lucy. "I got some really good shots. That was so exciting". Rachel smiled weakly and said nothing. The rest of the morning provided a wealth of opportunities for cameras to click and Rachel could not fail to be moved by the wildlife that the group saw. It was truly impressive. A small group of elephants bathed at the waterhole as a group of buffalo arrived and waited for the elephants to leave. As they did so the numbers of buffalo increased significantly and were then joined by about twenty or so zebras. At the same time at least four species of birds fluttered from tree to tree. The cameras clicked and whirred. The photographers babbled excitedly. The activity was continuous but Rachel remained quiet, nodding occasionally when spoken to, silent, lost in her thoughts.

She had hoped that the morning would have provided an alternative to the hunting safari and whilst the customers did not obviously take part in the killing, she was still appalled by the way they enjoyed it. In her mind it was clear that humans had no place in this environment and that most of the people, involved in both activities, lacked any real moral compass. Both sets of people were so wrapped up in their own immediate desires and activities that they gave little thought to the plight of the beasts they were filming.

Was she missing the point? Did she not understand human beings? Was she the only one to understand the stupidity and ignorance of the people involved? She was troubled. She did not understand her fellow man. Perhaps they were

right and she was wrong; humans were only animals after all. Maybe it was normal to enjoy the kill? Maybe she was being moralistic. These were nice people after all. They meant no harm.
Perhaps she was wrong.
She didn't think so.
Rachel looked at the people, the very nice people in her group and pitied them. The Land Rover arrived back at 2 p.m.. She thanked her hosts, said her goodbyes and drove back to the ranch and deleted the idea of an article exploring the benefits of photographic safaris. She had never felt so demoralised. She lay on her bed exhausted and immediately fell asleep.
Two hours later she woke and sat bolt upright in bed. There was no sign of sleep in her eyes. Her mind was clear. Anne was right. She had been all along. These people were mad, deluded and self-satisfied and they had to be stopped. She also saw her own delusion. These people, all of them, were not going to be stopped by reason. She saw that she had been a nice, middle class white lady who was angered by injustice but being angry was not enough. For a brief moment she stopped and thought of Andrew and the girls and the comfortable existence they had lived. It had been smashed in a moment and she was now about to leave what remnants that still remained for ever. Writing exposes was not enough.

People read an article and expressed outrage but it did no good. Shocking people with pictures of dead animals was futile. The readers were appalled and then carried on with their lives. They possibly mentioned the issue to their friends who then tut-tutted in shock before taking another sip of wine and moving on to the next topic of conversation.

All her respectable views crystallised and cracked before tumbling to the ground. All these people were deluded. The hunters who thought they were conserving wildlife, the angry who thought their anger was enough but the most significant delusion had been hers. She had believed that her writing would change the world. It was a lie. It was kill or be killed and there was no other way to stop them.

Her mouth was dry and her heart pounded as she stood up, strode across her room, flung open the door and leapt across the corridor. She banged on Anne's door. She opened it immediately as if she were expecting her. Rachel flung her arms around her and they embraced.

"You are right. You always were."

They stood there, locked together. Rachel then moved back and looked Anne straight in the eye before shrieking,

"No turning back!

Not now!

Not ever!"

CHAPTER 32

Rachel and Anne sat in Anne's room drinking their second bottle of wine. The wine had not touched Rachel's brain. She was trying to absorb what Anne had just told her. The "action", as she described it, would occur in two days time on Friday, one day before they were due to leave South Africa.

The more Rachel listened to Anne's plans the more she felt a little disappointed. Committing herself to such a dangerous and criminal act had been frightening, exciting and filled with purpose. Now facing up to the reality of what was about to happen had brought her down to earth. She had not thought it through properly. She had no rifle training. And as a result, she would not be directly involved in the "action".

Anne had asked her to visit Jonathan in his village, ostensibly to interview him about his new job as a ranger with the Government's Animal Protection Department. Originally Rachel had thought about doing a new interview with him as part of their visit. Now it was part of the plan.

"We want you to distract the police from us. They'll want to interview us all as we are here but spending time on you would take time and take the police down false lines of enquiry. Hopefully they will see that all the main people around the investigation who had not been killed will be two women on holiday and one Government employee with no known record of violence.

This will confuse the police who will have no real clue as to who could have done it. They will have no obvious motive to go on."

"But don't we want people to know why it was done? What's the point?"

"That will be taken care of."

"But how?"

"The less you know the less danger you will be in. Trust me."

Rachel suddenly felt unsure. She had committed herself in a moment of anger and frustration, of righteousness even but now she felt helpless and insignificant.

Anne saw the look of disappointment and reassured her.

"This is just the beginning. You are playing a very important part, believe me but give yourself time. Friday the hunting will begin. The guilty will be destroyed and you will be with us."

"Who is the hunter? I thought it was you."

Anne smiled,

"Is it you?"

"I can't say anything. Not at this moment."

"Did you shoot David? Please. I'm so confused and so want to be a part of this. Are you the hunter? Did you kill David?"
Anne sighed.
"I know I can trust you"
"Absolutely. I'm deadly serious. I told you "
"I shot David."
Rachel drew a deep intake of breath.
"He was a bully. He made my life a misery. I had to look at that poor animal's head on our wall every day. He laughed when I asked him to remove it and he hit me when I tried to do so."
"He hit you?"
"Many times. I couldn't take it anymore. I was at my wits end. He was so cruel. All these people are cruel."
Anne nodded slowly as if to re-affirm her point.
"I killed him."
"Do You feel any remorse?"
"Not one jot. He deserved it. They all deserve it."
Now Rachel understood who Anne was as a person and in the same moment she understood the person that she herself was becoming.
No turning back.
Not now.
Not ever.

CHAPTER 33

If Friday was going to be the all important day, Thursday was of no less significance. There was a lot of preparation to do to ensure Friday was a success. They had breakfast as normal between 6 and 6.30 am. Both Rachel and Anne smiled at Michael and Guy and exchanged pleasantries with Zach. It was surreal because if things were to go as planned all the people they were being polite to would be dead within 28 hours.

They did spend some time with Zach. They had planned the conversation. They needed to know what the plans were for the next two days but to avoid raising any suspicions caused by their unusual interest they had decided to ask about the activities every day. Rachel and Anne wanted to make it seem like an all-round, general conversation and one which didn't focus solely on Friday's activities.

"Today we are going down into the valley. We will walk along the river and spend time at the water hole. Tomorrow we're going further north than usual, into the hills. It's got quite lush up there and there are some buffalo," was all Zach would say. He seemed distracted. He had reason to be. The previous day he had received

another death threat. It was a simple statement which simply said,
"YOU'RE GOING TO DIE" in newspaper capitals. At first he had thought it wise to inform the police but had then decided against it. What could they do? The area was so vast it couldn't be patrolled on a regular basis and besides the staff had guns. They could defend themselves but as the week moved on, he had felt something, a tension that hadn't existed before.

His wife had mentioned something like this on several occasions throughout their married life and had frequently talked about how she could "feel" things.

She would say something like' "I felt someone pass by me today. Someone is watching me." Then something would happen a few days later and she would claim that it was linked to her earlier experiences which proved her instincts were correct.

Zach had always dismissed this as "women's nonsense" but today it was different. Someone or something was watching him. He could feel it. It was malignant, threatening with a sense of overpowering hatred. He shivered and dismissed it. He had to, otherwise it would defeat him. He couldn't allow that to happen but the quicker he dismissed it, the quicker it came back. It wasn't just watching him. It was following him. He was being hunted.

Zach had decided to keep his own counsel. He would trust no-one, not even those two nice ladies who seemed so harmless. The American had seemed harmless enough when she said she was trying to re-visit her husband's last hunting trip and the other one was just a reporter looking for a story but the first one had proved herself more than handy with a rifle when the lion attacked the Mexican whose name he couldn't remember. Was she all that she seemed?

His inability to remember the man's name had also bothered him. Normally he could remember all of his clients' names while they were at his ranch and many he still remembered long after they had gone. How could he forget his name especially after such a notable and recent event?

The fact was, he couldn't. He could see his face, the pain he suffered and the fear in his eyes but his name had gone from Zach's memory. Was this because he felt stressed? Was he anxious? He wouldn't admit to it. Concerned yes but anxious? Of course he was. He was "concerned" enough to put a pistol into a holster. He wanted it with him at all times and it would give him speed and mobility in handling a firearm that a rifle would not. Initially he had chosen a Luger hunting pistol but then had decided to add a Luger 9 instead. It was a much smaller 9mm pistol for closer targets and had a 15 round capacity; just enough to deal with anyone at closer range. He was frightened but ready. They were not going to destroy everything he had built without a fight. The trouble was he didn't know who they were.

It was time to leave. He went to his room and prepared his weapons.

If Zach was distracted, so were Rachel and Anne. "Further north, and to the hills can only mean," she hesitated, "these hills here". Her finger landed on the Lebombo mountain range shown on a map that was spread out on a large coffee table. Both of them were on their knees pouring over the details of the map. "There are three main routes that can be driven but they are miles apart. We have no way of working out which one the hunting party will take.

"If I were to hazard a guess it would be here, the one to the north but it's only a guess."

Anne paused. "Damn. It's a large area."

"Maybe we'll just have to hunt them then."

Anne smiled at her friend's newfound enthusiasm.

"How fit do you feel? No, we'll have to talk to Johnathan. We shall have to do a reccy.

I've spoken to Zach and he's agreed to lend us Johnathan for the day. We'll go out in an hour after everyone's left. Zach thinks we're doing some late sight-seeing before we leave but I don't want him to see us heading north.

It took almost two hours before they entered a vast grassland plain which led to the foothills. The main hills were not particularly high, standing at around 2000 feet but it was nevertheless a beautiful sight.

'It's very open," Rachel had said the same words that Anne was about to speak.

"Any vehicle approaching would be easily spotted."

"We can go by another route and come round on them," said Johnathan. "We would not be seen and could reach the top in good time."

Rachel stared at Johnathan "but I thought I was coming to see you.'

'You are."

"Anne can't do that by herself."

Anne continued to stare at the vista in front of them, "I'll be alright."

Rachel felt a sudden dread come over her. Not only was the whole exercise a dangerous one with regard to the human aspect but there were dangerous animals out there in a very isolated area.

"This is not possible.'

"She'll be alright." Jonathan spoke with more force than he had ever done before.

"She'll be alright," he repeated calmly.

Rachel looked at him and then switched her stare to Anne before returning her stare to Johnathan.

"Clearly there are things that I don't know about."
"And that's how it needs to stay for the moment," Anne interrupted. "We need to protect you, for now. We have been planning this for months. As I told you before, you are protecting us by helping to provide a distraction to the police and," she hesitated, "You are my friend."
There was a long pause. Rachel nodded her head.
"OK. I can see you know what you are doing. I think. I am committed, you know. I just want to help."
"Believe me, you are doing."
They drove around the escarpment and parked the vehicle out of sight of the main route and then began a hill climb at a rapid pace. Despite their speed it took them half an hour to reach the top. Rachel collapsed, exhausted. The three of them sat on a large rock at the top of the hill. They could not see their own vehicle. About four hundred feet beneath them beneath them they could see a group of buffalo grazing.
"This is where they will come towards us here. They will park there. I've done it before. This is perfect," said Johnathan who was assuming an authority he had never shown before.
They sat there surveying the scene as if it were an outing. Rachel sat up. She realised she was not anywhere near as fit as her comrades and she was not ready to engage in

their actions but she had started to think that, someday in the future, this may all provide good material for a book.

Anne began to walk about the hilltop looking at possible vantage points and assessing possible dangers in the terrain.

Rachel turned to Johnathan. "I'm still coming to see you in your village tomorrow?"

"Yes of course."

"I'll be there in the afternoon. At 2pm."

"Yes as agreed."

"Will Anne be OK tomorrow? How did she become so strong, so determined?"

"Life can take you places sometimes. Places you never imagined you would go. She is on a mission, completely absorbed by it. She has to complete that which she is determined to do. She believes in what she is doing and the only thing that will stop her is death."

"I am beginning to realise that. When my husband and children died, I was so angry but now I'm not quite certain where I am."

"We know and it's OK to feel like that. You've been through a hard time and you're still working things out."

"I just know that life isn't fair. It's corrupt and murderous and we dress it up as if everything is perfectly normal but it's not. Our leaders present themselves as respectable and they are until they get caught. Then it's described as a

shock but it's not. We have a vote to make certain it's all above board and legal but it's not. Elected leaders, judges, media people, priests, they all lie. The people who police it all are just as bad. That's why nothing changes. They pretend that things will change but nothing really does. It's all stifled in procedures and inquiries. In my country nearly a hundred people died in a fire at a block of flats because the builders fitted cheap, faulty cladding. No-one's been prosecuted. I thought that justice simply took a long time but it doesn't. It's corrupt, a masquerade.
I thought I would be afraid but I'm not worried. I wouldn't be here if I was worried but there are so many things to get right in your head before you can be as certain as Anne. Can I ask you about one last doubt I have?"

"Of course. I'll try to help."

"I have obviously rejected the idea of hunting. I've fallen out with photographic safaris but what is your objection to farming wild animals? Do they not increase the number of animals?"

"You should not be deceived by what's happening at Zach's ranch. It all looks very clean and well managed and it is but there is a lot going on that is not seen and other places aren't as good in the care of animals. Farming for hunting is presented to the public as a nice alternative but there are many unpleasant things happening."

"What kind of things are you talking about?"

"China banned tiger hunting in 1993 because the number of tigers in the wild had fallen to about 4000. So, suppliers of bones to Asia turned their eyes towards Africa and several wild animal breeding centres now supply bones to China."

"So, this is not just about hunting?"

It's about making money any way you can." Jonathan gripped the steering wheel and shook his head. "They have no respect for the animals; none at all. In some places, the lions are kept in cages and when they are shot they are shot through the ears instead of the eyes."

"Why?"

"Because it does less damage to the skull. They get more money if the lion's skull is intact, so they use a lower calibre gun."

"Does that make a difference?"

"Yes it does. A shot to the ear does less damage to the skins. They breed the lions and organise hunts in fenced-off areas so that the animals can't escape. They sell their heads as trophies and also the skins. After the meat is boiled off, the bones are then shipped out to Asia. No one can tell if the bones come from an animal that died in the wild or one of the farmed animals."

"Does Zach's hunt do this?"

Jonathan remained silent.

"This is my employment. Zach is my boss. He won't let me say anything. If he found out, I'd lose my job." He paused, "It goes on everywhere here we have Government permits but many operate without them. They don't care. The money is so good it makes the risk of getting caught worthwhile. They are just like poachers. They have almost destroyed the tiger species. They have damaged the lion and when they have difficulties getting hold of enough animals they breed them themselves in order to kill them. Who knows which of the lions who end up in China, came from a real hunt or a playground?

Most people who do the poaching are poor black people like me. It's horrible but they do it for the money because they are desperate. The organisers are rich white people. It's the same with safaris and some people are getting very rich out of the misery of those in poverty and the poor animals they live near. You can't separate poverty from hunting.

I wish it would go back to the old days when game was plentiful and tribes people hunted when necessary."

"But hasn't that caused animal populations to drop over the last century as the human population has grown?"

"This is nonsense. Safaris have destroyed or damaged populations, not the real hunter. There's a lot of space out there where man and animals can still live together if it is managed properly. In my opinion there is no alternative.

No, no alternatives. The killing has to stop. The killers have to be taken out.

As they finished speaking Anne came back from round a huge boulder. They had not heard her at all. It was clear immediately that it would be easy to mount a surprise attack.

"I'm ready."

"So am I," said Jonathan.

"So am I," said Rachel.

"Whatever you want me to do. I'm ready."

They drove home and went to sleep early. They drank no alcohol. They needed to be ready for whatever tomorrow was going to bring them.

CHAPTER 34

Next morning Zach left after an early breakfast accompanied by Michael and Guy. The ranch was unnervingly quiet and still. At about 7.00am she watched the small number of catering staff depart to their villages. They were not required until the late afternoon when they would prepare the evening meal. Anne had still not appeared by 8.00am. She had made a brief appearance at 6.00am and had been at pains to ensure that all the staff knew she was feeling unwell and was returning to her bed. Rachel waited until 9.00am, conscious of the fact that she would have to leave in the next few minutes to see Johnathan and his family as arranged.

She knocked on Anne's door to check on her. There was no reply. Quietly she entered the room. Small stripes of light from the louvred windows strafed the walls. Rachel's eyes were adjusting to the light, her ears concerned about the silence. Rachel knew Anne took tablets for depression since David's death. Her prescriptions would be recorded on her medical file back home and would be useful evidence to back up her story about being ill but had the stress of what she was planning taken its toll? She opened the blinds. There was no sign of Anne.

Rachel was surprised at first. Why had she not told Rachel that she would be leaving without seeing her? Rachel went to the yard. There was only one vehicle left for her to travel to Johnathan's. Anne had gone. Rachel stood on the steps. Something momentous was about to happen. She had a small part in it but was not certain how it would all unfold. Perhaps that was for the best. Perhaps Anne simply wanted to ensure that absolutely no-one, not even her ally saw her go. Rachel spent the rest of the morning packing and preparing to leave. Everything had to look as normal as possible. At one o'clock she got herself ready and left.

CHAPTER 35

Zach and his party arrived at the foot of the mountain range at the same point that Johnathan had stopped the previous day. A strong breeze had been blowing through the night which had made it impossible to spot the earlier tyre tracks left by yesterday's visitors. Thankfully for the hunting party that breeze had now dissipated and the early morning was clear and sunny. It was a good day for hunting but that strange feeling of fear had returned to Zach. He scanned the ridge tops and lower-level boulders but saw nothing. Nevertheless, he took the precaution of equipping himself with his pistols.

He led them on foot for just over half a mile following some buffalo tracks. The buffalos had been spotted two days earlier by trackers. He didn't expect that they would have moved too far because of the lushness of the vegetation and the proximity of small streams flowing from the mountain into a small water hole. It was ideal. After an hour they spotted four females and one large, ageing bull. "Perfect," thought Zach.

He pointed to the bull.

"That's your target," he hissed.

In her enthusiasm Madeleine stood up, took aim and fired. The bullet missed and scattered the animals. The other members of the party stood up to see where the animals had gone and for a second, did not notice that Madeleine had fallen backwards. She was lying motionless on the ground. Karl turned and to his horror, saw blood pouring from his wife's forehead. A rifle had fired at precisely the same moment that Madeleine had discharged her weapon. He gasped and moved towards her when a second shot hit him in the left temple, killing him instantly. He fell over her body and the settling dust collected over him.

"Get down!" screamed Zach. Guy and Michael needed no invitation as all three of them hid behind the Ranger. Zach fumbled for his phone but realised he'd left it in the cabin when he put on his pistol belt. He turned to his two clients but they shook their heads. It normally wasn't a good idea to carry mobile phones on a hunt. There was always a risk that one would ring and spook the animals.

"Listen!" Zach barked, "We're under attack. We are going to have to defend ourselves and stop that guy."

The men nodded, "Who is it?"

"I've no fuckin' idea and for now it doesn't matter. We have to get out of here alive. We need to spread out and make ourselves a more diverse target. Can one of you dash behind that rock? He pointed to a large 6-foot by 6-foot rock some 10 yards to their right.

"I'm a vet.," said Guy. "I'll do it. We don't have a choice."

"We'll cover."

As soon as he moved, both Zach and Michael stood and returned fire. Immediately a shot returned and hit Michael in the head. The force of the impact turned him round and his rifle fired as he fell backwards onto the ground, dead. The shot from Michael's rifle wounded Zach who fell to his knees. Guy dived behind the rock and its relative safety. He could only crouch and stare at the disfigured head of his friend.

"Fuck, fuck, fuck!" screamed Guy who was trying not to panic. His claim to being a vet had been bravado. He had served in the catering corps. He had only fired a gun at an unarmed animal. Now someone was shooting at him.

The gunfire stopped. There were no more targets for now. Guy tried to scan the hills before him but could see no movement. He turned to look at Zach but he had disappeared. Guy could see nothing. He threw his cap out in an attempt to draw fire but that failed. Then he put his rifle along the side of the rock and fired in the general direction of the shots but again there was no response. After a twenty-minute stand-off he decided to retreat. Guy left the cover of his rock and began to run. Immediately a bullet hit him in the right shoulder from the front. He lay on the floor stunned. He had been shot from the other direction. How had the attacker got behind him? Were there two of them? His mind raced as his body lay still. He

tried to prop himself up when he heard footsteps walking towards him. Then a figure appeared in front of him.
"What? Why? Why you?"
"I am the Hunter." the Hunter said.
"What?"
"What does it feel like to be hunted?"
"What?" was all he could muster. "I've come to dispatch you. That's what they call it. Isn't it?"
"Please. I have children."
The hunter laughed.
"So does nearly every animal you kill.``
Guy was aware that he was bleeding heavily. He stared in disbelief at the changing colour of his shirt and then he fell into unconsciousness.
The hunter raised the rifle.
"Stop!"
"Don't move!"
"Drop your rifle and put your hands up!"
Zach was standing there holding his small Luger 9.
He was covered in blood and panting heavily.
"You fucking bitch! I knew there was something phoney about you. All that talk about your husband's last happy place. Where's that other bitch? Is she part of it as well?
"If you mean Rachel. No she's not."

Anne was trying to sound defiant but all the time she was aware of the stream of urine trickling down her legs. Zach saw it and laughed.

"Ha, you are not that fuckin tough. Fucking women make me fucking sick.'

"What are you going to do?"

"Well, I can't take you in can I? I'm not going to make it. I'll bleed to death before I get to the police station. I'm going to fucking shoot you."

As he raised his arm it shook with the effort but the gun was still pointing at her.

"Fucking b...."

Just then a bullet struck his jaw, shattering it. He fell to the ground and banged his head on a small rock killing him instantly.

The dust settled and the ground was still but there were no sounds of birds.

Anne fell to the ground and sobbed. She cried from fear and from the release of tension, the knowledge that everything had been achieved. She stopped crying when she heard the sound of footsteps. She looked up and smiled. Standing in front of her was the figure of her colleague and saviour.

"You took your time!"

"I couldn't get a clear shot. The truck partially obscured my view. When he lifted his hand, his head tipped forward and I could see him. It was a good clean shot."
They embraced.
They had achieved everything they wanted. All they had to do was check that they left no equipment and no obvious footprints.

CHAPTER 36

Meanwhile Rachel had spent the afternoon with Jonnathan. She wanted to take some more photographs of his village. Jonathan and his wife Lerato were most hospitable. They sat and drank Rooibos tea and talked about family life. Since her last visit Johnathan and his wife had had their third child. Their house was much bigger than she remembered. It had running water and electricity supplied by a generator and a solar panel.

Jonathan had some amazing and significant news. He was leaving the hunting ranch.

He had got a job as a ranger with the Government's Animal Protection Agency.

"How do you feel about that Lerato?'

"I am happy for him. He had started to hate working at the Ranch. We have moved back to the village because we want to live a traditional life like that of our people. That must mean that helping the white hunters has to stop. We are improving our farming and we get good food now from our land. It is getting better all the time. I am very happy but I do worry about him. A ranger's job can be dangerous, you know."

"She worries about me all the time," laughed Johnathan. "Mostly I will be helping farmers to build stronger compounds to keep lions away from their cattle and educating children in school."

"Yes but sometimes.'

"Only sometimes," he interrupted. "Only sometimes, I promise."

Lerato smiled but Rachel could see her fear and thought about how unnecessarily unpleasant life could be and it was all caused by poverty and its alter ego, greed.

She took some more photographs to show how Johnathan's life was developing and the news that he had decided to leave the Safari would provide a good angle for a follow up story to her first but then decided that any follow up story would be affected by the events occurring right at that moment. Then it dawned on her that that was precisely the point. The police would not be able to prove her involvement if, at the time, she was planning an article about the Safari ranch.

As she smiled at Anne's detailed planning a mobile phone rang. Jonathan took it out of his pocket.

"Yes. Yes. Good. OK. We are on our way now."

"Lerato we have to go now."

"Is anything the matter?"

"No, no, not at all."

They got in the Land Rover.

"Anything wrong?" asked Rachel.

"No, no, far from it. It's all done."

"It's over?"

"No, it's just begun. We have to rendezvous with Anne in half an hour to pick up a package."

"A package, what do you mean?"

"You'll see. Anne has to get back before any staff return. She said she was too ill to join the hunt, remember?"

"Of course. Well, I said I'd do anything to help."

After about twenty minutes Johnathan turned off the main road onto a dirt track. Rising in front of them but some distance away, were the hills they had visited the previous day.

"You can see for miles."

"Good it's such a big area for the police to cover. The bodies will take some time to discover and they probably won't be found until we report them missing but we can't take any chances. The most important thing is to get Anne back and to deal with the package. They carried on for another ten minutes before they came to a small water hole surrounded by trees. Sitting on a rock was Anne and next to her, to Rachel's utter amazement, was Kyle.

He didn't look any different. He stood up and grinned at her. Rachel, forgetting that any intimacy they may have shared had been in her dreams, got out of the Land Rover, ran up to him and flung her arms around him.

"I thought you were dead!"

"Well nearly but not yet."

"I am so pleased to see you."

"So am I."

They stood beaming at each other for a brief eternity before Anne said, "I have to go."

Anne and Kyle embraced once more.

Anne turned to Rachel, "I am going back to the ranch in the Land Rover now with Johnathan. Kyle, here are my rifle, boots and mobile. Have you got yours together?"

"Yes, all in the bag."

"You know what to do?"

"Absolutely, no problem. No trace." He smiled.

"Sorry, just checking."

She turned to Rachel. "You need to deliver Kyle and then get back straight away."

The dust from the Land Rover had still not settled as Kyle threw the Ranger into gear.

"I will be picked up," he checked his watch, "in 40 minutes". They drove back down the track, turned left on to the main road that Rachel recognised. After twenty minutes they turned into a filling station and waited.

"I was told you were dead'

"I nearly was."

"What happened?"

"I was a Ranger, part of the Government's animal protection Department. I worked in Special Operations. We had information about a group of poachers entering the

north of Limpopo from Kenya. These are well organised groups and they operate across borders often organised from within South Africa. They're after rhino horns and elephant tusks, that kind of thing.
We found them and cornered them. There was a shootout but we were outnumbered. Three of my comrades were killed and I was shot in the shoulder. I fell into a ravine and was badly banged about. Somehow, I managed to hide myself in a bush. I don't know how they didn't see me but I could see them, him."
"Who?"
He turned slowly to face her and said,
"Zach."
"Oh my God!"
"He was the organiser. I sat there and just didn't breathe and then I thought to myself
'Were you part of the gang that killed my parents?' Of course, I had no proof."
"No."
"But from that moment on I determined I would do everything in my power to stop all these activities."
"How did you get away?"
"I passed out. I don't know how long I was there. It was getting dark when I climbed out. I managed to summon help from a friend. From then on, I officially died.

'Probably taken by animals. There was no trace left', was the official announcement"
"How did you team up with Anne?"
"Ah well that's another story. Don't forget I don't exist."
They stared at each other. She was about to kiss him but a Ford saloon pulled alongside and ended the moment.
"Look after yourself," she whispered.
He smiled and spoke gently. "I'll try. Take care. Get back to the ranch now."
With that he got out of the Ranger and climbed into the car. His departure took but a moment; the dust took an age to settle.

CHAPTER 37

It took Rachel twenty minutes to drive back to the ranch. She unlocked the main gate and parked the Ranger alongside the Land Rover. There was no one around and the place was eerily quiet. Rachel collected her notebook and recorder together with her mobile and shut the door. At that moment Anne appeared in the doorway. They stood and stared at each other before running to greet and embrace one another. Anne's hair was still wet from her shower.

"We did it" exclaimed Rachel. "This place will never be the same."

"No it won't but there's still a long way to go. What we have done is going to terrify the hunting industry but we have to deal with the police and press. We say as little as possible. That's the secret to lying well."

They smiled and embraced again. As they did, a vehicle stopped outside the gates. Anele, one of the cooks, had arrived to prepare the evening meal. She smiled as she entered the courtyard.

"Good evening Ma'am. Are you better?"

"Yes, thanks I am much better. I've had a long sleep and I've just got up and had a shower."

"Oh good, well I must get on. They'll be arriving back soon."

Anne and Rachel followed her back into the main entrance and turned into Anne's room. They sat there drinking tea. There was no place for alcohol.

"You've got photographs and recordings to show where you and Johnathan were?"

"Yes."

"Good. We're all set. I'll phone Zach's phone when the staff raise concerns. After a while we'll inform the police. By the time they arrive it will be dark. They won't be able to launch a search until morning. We simply have to wait."

It was a long wait. Anne made a point of occasionally going to the main gate as if she were trying to see any sign of a return. Then she would check her watch to indicate a growing concern should any of the staff had seen her.

At 5.30 pm she was approached by Anele.

"They are not back ma'am."

"No, something must have happened. There has been no phone call?"

"No ma'am, there is only one land line in the office."

"Mmm I'll go and ring Mr.Baas..

Anne entered the office and picked up the phone. She needed to do this to show to the police that she had been trying to contact the hunting party. There was no reply.

She waited. She was about to put the phone down when to her horror someone answered.
"Hello?"
A voice coughed and choked out a reply. "Hello?"
It was obvious that the person was struggling to use the phone.
"Hello!" urged Anne, "Who is that?"
"It's Guy".

CHAPTER 38

Anne dropped the phone but quickly regathered it. She tried to appear calm
"Guy, where are you?"
"They're all dead."
Anne's heart was racing.
"Who are?"
"Everyone. Someone shot them."
"I'll phone the police."
There was no reply.
"Guy? Guy!"
It was obvious he could not reply. Either the phone was dead or he was. Maybe it had been a last rally by a dying man. Maybe he had already phoned the police?
She could do nothing except call the police earlier than intended and wait.
Meanwhile, some seventy miles away, darkness fell on the South African border with Botswana. Two men set out to cross the Limpopo river in an inflatable dinghy. Halfway across they dropped two bags, weighted with bricks, quietly into the depths. They then continued across into Botswana. They dragged their boat out of the water and left it some way into the forest. The men cleaned the boat, removed their equipment and disappeared.

CHAPTER 39

It took the police an hour to arrive. The young officer was tall, tanned and very blond. He looked down at Anne with a suggestion that he already regarded her as guilty of something. It was quite intimidating. He did not give his name. The two women showed him into the dining area. He did not sit down.
"Who is in charge here?"
"No-one is. I'm a paying guest as is Rachel." The officer turned to Rachel and gave her the same look he had directed towards Anne. He took details from Anne.
She explained why they had phoned the police.
"You say a man called Guy phoned and said everyone was dead?"
"No, I phoned him."
"Why?"
"Because, as I said, the party of hunters from this Safari organisation had not returned."
"You didn't go on the hunt?"
"No, I was ill."
"What was wrong with you?"
Anne sighed "Look is this relevant? I phoned the owner of this establishment because it was getting dark and the staff had the evening meal ready. There was no sign of the

group coming back. It was getting dark.It was unusual. We were concerned."

"Who are we?"

"Myself, the staff and my friend, Rachel

The officer continued taking notes.

"Look shouldn't you be organising a search?"

"Do you know where they went?"

"No. "Zach said something about a mountain range up north."

"Right, that makes it very difficult. Will the staff know?"

"I have no idea. I don't run this place. You'll have to ask them."

"Wait here."

The constable left Anne to speak to the staff. He returned a few moments later.

"They are all catering staff. They don't know anything about the trips out. Are there any other staff?"

"There are a couple of guides but I couldn't contact them."

"Why?"

"I don't really know them. They should be here in the morning. Shouldn't you be organising a search?"

"Well, it's difficult enough in the dark but we don't even know where they are. Up north is a very vague description. They could be anywhere. First of all, have you got the number you rang earlier when the man answered?"

"It's in the office on the desk."

"Show me."

The three of them went into the reception. Anne pointed to the piece of paper with Zach's number on it. The police officer rang it. Anne and Rachel held their breath. Eventually a voice answered. For a moment their hearts jumped.

"Sorry the number you are ringing is unavailable."

Rachel and Anne both took a deep breath unseen by the officer.

"Right, I'll phone this in to my commander. He'll decide what happens next. No doubt you'll be visited in the morning and if they don't show up they'll organise a search first thing. Please let us know if they return."

The phone rang. The two women stared at each other, frozen.

Rachel saw the alarm in Anne's eyes. Anne saw the same fear in Rachel's.

The officer saw it in both of them.

The women did not move and the phone kept on ringing.

The officer picked it up. He switched it to the speaker.

"Hello?"

There was no reply.

Then a voice whispered slowly, "Hello. Who is that?."

"This is the police. Who am I speaking to.?"

"Guy. I phoned before. I need help."

"Guy who?"

"He's one of the party," snapped Rachel.
"Where are you?"
"Where are you?"
"Don't know. I've been shot"
"Who shot you?"
Rachel and Anne could only stare at the phone, gripped in fear.
The constable was watching them.
"They are coming to get me."
"Who are they?"
"Hyenas. They came before but I have run out of bullets."
The sound of growling and laughing became stronger.
"Get away! Get away you bastards!" The awful laugh of the hyenas intensified.
The screams were terrifying. They lasted a few seconds only and then stopped. The only sounds they could hear were the sounds of cracking bones and tearing flesh. The officer put the phone down. There was nothing they could do.
It was as if nature had gained its revenge on the hunters.

CHAPTER 40

The two women woke up the next morning at about 7.00am. They entered a very subdued dining room. Only Anele was present. They ate their breakfast in total silence.

Anele came into the room to offer more coffee.

"Something very bad has happened, has it not ma'am?"

Anne took a deep breath and smiled gently. "I'm afraid it would appear so."

She saw the sadness in Anele's eyes.

"When will we hear something?"

"I presume the police will tell us as soon as they find our people."

"Yes, I do hope so but I fear that the police are not very efficient."

"I'm sure they are doing their best. The problem is that no-one seems to know exactly where they went. Mr. Baas just told me 'Up north but I have no idea where."

"Yes it is very strange."

At that precise moment 3 police vehicles swept into the courtyard and parked outside the main entrance. Within seconds they had entered the dining room and asked to speak to Anne.

"Mrs.Mulhern, I'm Captain Handre Stranksky of the Polokwane police department. I'm afraid we have some bad news for you. We have found the vehicles from this Safari club and I'm afraid there are a number of fatalities."
There was a gasp and a cry as Anele ran out of the kitchen and shouted to the other staff. There was a commotion outside as staff ran to each other. Anne had not anticipated this reaction and it shook her. People's jobs were at stake. It wasn't just a question of the morals of the hunting safari.
"We are at this moment trying to assess the situation. Can you tell us how many people were in the group?"
"There was one woman and" she paused while she counted on her fingers "Guy, Michael, Zach er, Mr. Baas and the woman's husband. I'm sorry I don't remember his name."
"So that's five people in total?"
'Yes I think so. We didn't actually see them go out did we?"
Rachel nodded her head.
"You told the officer that Mr. Baas had told you that he was heading north?"
"Yes."
"But you didn't ask how many people were going? Why not?"
"Er, I didn't think to."

"Mm OK."

"'Sergeant Le Roux!"

A middle-aged, burly man with a bald head filled the doorway.

"Captain?"

"Please radio the search team and tell them they are looking for five bodies in total.

The sergeant withdrew but returned within seconds.

"Captain, they have found four bodies so far and they're still searching."

Anne exchanged a panic-ridden glance which Stransky saw.

"Do you have a problem?"

"I don't want anyone to suffer. It's so upsetting. Why would anyone want to shoot them?"

" Who said they'd been shot?"

"Well I just presumed. How else would they all be killed?"

"Please don't presume anything Mrs Mulhern."

For a moment this panicked Anne but she quickly recovered her composure. "Guy told me they had been shot. I told your officer."

Stransky said nothing but looked directly at Anne and smiled.

"We shall establish the cause of death as soon as possible."

At that moment Sergeant Le Roux's radio crackled loudly.

"Yes? Yes, OK. Thanks. Captain they have found remains of a fifth body several yards away from the others and yes they have all been shot." He looked knowingly at the two women. There was an awkward silence. The two women lowered their eyes.
"Well that settles that then. Right,I need a room to act as a base for the investigation into their deaths."
He looked at Anne.
"I have no authority here. I'm just a paying guest."
"Is there no-one to assume authority?"
"Well there's Johnathan."
"Who's he?"
He's Zach's assistant I suppose. He drives one of the vehicles and assists on the hunts."
"Where is he?"
"He's not here."
"Well that's obvious. I asked where he was."
Rachel did not like Stransky's manner but reasoned that he was not paid to be liked. He frightened her. She had to be on her guard, to say as little as possible. It was obvious that they were still in danger and that their "hunt", for that is what it had been, was far from over. She realised that, although she had not been involved in the actual killings she could destroy everything with a few careless words.
"I went to his village but he drove there and back and I can't remember its name."

"What's his name?"
"Johnathan. I'm afraid I don't know his surname."
"What was the name of the village?"
"I don't know. As I said he drove there and back. We're just visitors. We are not part of this organisation. The staff might know."
Just then a vehicle arrived at the front of the building. Jonathan"s large frame got out. He fixed a surprised stare on the police cars.
Stransky turned to Rachel, "Is that Johnathan?"
"Yes.'
He went to him straight away.
"Hello I'm Captain Stransky."
"What's happening?"
"I'm afraid that several people from this ranch have been murdered."
Johnathan was very convincing in his responses. He took Stransky to the office and helped the police gain access to the computer files and the victims' records. The police would have to gain details of next of kin and inform them. Officers spent the morning examining their rooms but found nothing that could give a lead as to why they had been murdered. Checks on the police records in the victims' individual countries showed nothing except the odd speeding ticket. There was nothing to suggest any motive for their being killed.

Stransky sat in his office the following day. He was talking over the details with his Commander, Francois Muller. "They were either shot by a gang of poachers or robbers or," he hesitated "by a group of anti-hunting activists. We know he had received a couple of death threats."
Muller had been aware of the death threats but had considered them to be the work of cranks.
"There's been no evidence that these people were organised in any way."
"Until now?"
"We've had no intelligence whatsoever."
"It's more than likely that they've come across a gang of poachers after the same game that they were after."
Stransky was uncomfortable with his Commander's instant dismissal of the possibility of a motivated attack by some sort of anti-hunt group but it was true that they had no concrete evidence worth going on.
"That leaves us with the two women," Stransky suggested.
"How likely?"
"Not very but there is one thing."
"Yes?"
"The American woman. Her husband was on a hunt here a couple of years ago." He was murdered. I've been onto her local police. It turns out they had no clues as to a likely suspect but he had received death threats and had actually moved house as a result. They were aware of domestic

problems and when they visited their house after his death all the reminders of his hunting, pictures, trophies, everything had been removed. They never had any proof but she was considered 'a person of interest'."
"What about the English woman?"
"She is a reporter for a well-known English newspaper." She did a big article on safari hunting. She got a lot of plaudits for it. She's also done a few articles on the environment and is involved with a couple of groups in England."
"My, you have been busy."
"OK you'd better bring them in for questioning."
"One other thing. The black guy. He's leaving. We found a letter of resignation on file in the office"
"Is he now? Bring him in as well."
"There's one final thing."
Muller sighed, "Yes?"
"Constable Kriege reported that when the phone rang in the office both the women looked terrified."
"And?"
"It was his impression that they were frightened of the call.
"You mean..
"It might come to nothing but it might suggest some knowledge?
"Mmm; well done."

CHAPTER 41

Two days after they should have left the country Anne and Rachel were driven into Polokwane police station in separate police vehicles, each escorted by two police officers. Although Rachel had not been involved in any of the violence, it was, nevertheless, a nerve-wracking experience.

Anne,on the other hand, showed no sense of stress. She had expected to be called in. She was prepared and confident. Her confidence did not waiver when she saw Johnathan in the waiting area.

The waiting area contained four plastic chairs that sat uncomfortably against the walls of the room. Except it wasn't actually a room, more a large alcove that lay off a long narrow corridor whose walls were punctured by a series of dark blue doors. The corridor was dingy. The pale yellow walls had not been painted in years and appeared to wilt under the mounting heat.

Rachel was less assured, even though she had been fully briefed on what to say it still felt as if the three of them were being hunted down, as if the police were closing in for the kill. They nodded to each other as they sat down but said nothing, fully aware that anything they might say would be relayed back to Captain Stransky by the attending constable.

A ceiling fan whirred lazily above them in a half-hearted attempt to reduce the temperature that was climbing steadily.

After fifteen minutes, Stransky opened one of the doors.

"Mrs. Hunter? Please come in."

Stransky invited Rachel to sit down. He faced her across a plain table with a white melamine top. He switched on the recorder and spoke into it.

"Captain Handre Stransky at Polokwane Central Police Station. Interview with Mrs. Rachel Hunter re murders at Lebombo, 15th March.2019."

He looked at Rachel and smiled briefly. She was tense but that was only to be expected. A nice middle class lady like her would probably never have been in a police station, let alone one as dingy and dismal as this one. It depressed him, let alone people who were potential suspects of having committed a crime. She didn't look like a criminal. She was very attractive, obviously intelligent and educated with strong, engaging eyes. Could a woman like her have committed such a brutal set of murders? Anyone would think it highly unlikely but he had seen many unlikely scenarios in his twenty years in the force. He wasn't going to be deceived by her good looks and sophistication. If she had any involvement he would not let an image fool him,

He would find out, one way or another whether these women were involved. He turned to her.

"Mrs. Hunter. Can you explain to me why you are here in South Africa at this time?"

"I was asked to come by my friend Anne. She lost her husband a couple of years ago. He was murdered."

"Oh that's terrible. Did they catch the murderer?"

"As far as I know, no."

"Do you know why he was killed?"

"Anne told me that he was getting death threats about his hunting exploits. That's all I know."

"They didn't manage to catch the killer?"

"As I said I don't think so."

"What were you planning to do whilst you were here?"

"I was going to keep Anne company. I also thought I'd take an opportunity to report on the hunting," she hesitated, "industry and see how things had changed since I wrote my article."

"Why did you hesitate when you used the word "industry?"

"Well it's not really an industry is it?"

"What would you call it?"

"I don't know. How about a money making operation?'

"You don't approve, do you?"

"Have you read my article?"

"Yes."

She was surprised."

"Really?"

"Well, it's not that difficult. You're a journalist. I typed in your name on the internet and it came up, articles as well. You got some awards for it I understand?"

"Yes."

"So you disapprove of hunting?"

"Hunting for fun. Yes."

" Do you disapprove enough to kill hunters?"

"That's ridiculous. I've never handled a gun in my life. My article was balanced and professional and I never had any complaints from the hunting" she hesitated again, "industry."

"Can you account for your movements on the day the murders were committed?"

"I stayed in in the morning and went to visit Jonathan, one of the staff at the ranch in the afternoon."

"Why?"

"I visited his home last time I was here. I wanted to do a piece on family life in an African village. I had met his wife and I thought I'd pay her a visit whilst I was here. I came back just before Anele arrived to cook tea. She can vouch for me being here. You can ask her."

"Thanks, I will." Stransky paused and then said, "Right. OK. Thank you. That's all for now.

"I can go? When can we make arrangements to go home?

"We'll contact you if we need to speak to you again. It will be in the next couple of days."

Rachel was surprised. She had feared the outcome of this interview but in actual fact it had been quite straightforward and surprisingly quick.

For his part Stransky was less interested in the British woman. The American was the key. Her husband was dead. According to American police she was regarded as a person of interest. She had a motive but they had no proof and the case had remained open. He didn't want that fate to befall his investigation. He finished his notes and went to the door and called out, "Mrs Mulhern? Anne entered the room calmly. She was well prepared for this and had rehearsed her story several times. She smiled slowly at Stransky and waited for him to invite her to sit down.

"Please sit down. Now you live in Eugene,Oregon in the USA?"

"Yes."

"And you have been there for how many years ? "

"Just two. Since my husband was killed."

"Yes I'm very sorry to hear that and I can't avoid asking questions about that. I understand that, as yet, they have not apprehended anyone?"

"No."

"That must be very upsetting."

"It would be useful to find his killers. We could have some closure and also there is always the threat that he could strike again ."
"Do you mean, at you?"
"Of course."
Do you think he might?"
"I was on the hunting trip with him."
"Mmm. Don't you think that by coming here it might make any potential killer think that you are still hunting?"
Anne paused.
"I didn't think of that. I came here for remembrance."
"I thought you and your husband had a troubled marriage?"
"Who said that?"
"Your local police said that you told them."
"Lots of marriages have troubles."
"Yes but most of them don't end up in the husband being shot down as if he'd been hunted."
At this Anne broke down in tears.
Stransky watched her carefully. Were they real tears? If they weren't she was a bloody good actress.
"I'm sorry Mrs Mulhern but five people are dead; six including your husband. All of them were hunters and that's the only known link between them. You are in the vicinity when killings took place in two different countries. Both your husband and the owner of the safari

park received written death threats cut out from newspapers in exactly the same way."

Anne gathered herself together.

"Did you kill your husband?"

'No!'

"Did you organise his killing?

Anne spoke softly, "No I had no involvement."

"Did you kill Zach Baas?"

"No!"

Did you kill Madeleine and Karl Johnson: a couple with three young grandchildren?"

"No, I did not."

"Did you kill Michael and Guy Brodie?"

Anne spoke calmly and softly. She knew that he was trying to ramp the pressure up on her. She looked him straight in the eye.

"No. I have killed no one. Nothing."

Stransky spoke softly.

"I have Mr. Baas's diary here. It records the daily activities of the guests.

It refers to an event last week when one of the guests was mauled by a lion."

Stransky read directly from it.

"The screams from Manuel were awful. It was very disturbing and scared the shit out of everyone but Mrs. Mulhern calmly stood up, took aim and fired three quick rounds into the lion's back killing him instantly. What fine shooting; it definitely saved the man's life."

Stransky closed the cover of the diary and looked at Anne. "You said you hate hunting and you'd had only basic gun training yet you stay calm and composed enough to kill a very dangerous beast that's endangering human life when others around you panic. You are so good as to draw praise from a seasoned gun handler."

He smiled at her. "That's very impressive. Hardly the actions of someone who hates guns."

"I was amazed at myself. I knew how to handle a gun. I never denied that. I heard a man screaming for his life and reacted in a way I never imagined I would react, ever in my life."

"It's lucky for that man that you did." Stransky smiled, clasped his fingers and looked at Anne for a few moments. "Mrs Mulhern, did you kill your husband?

Anne shook her head and whispered, "No."

"Did you kill those people?"

Again, she nodded and whispered the same word, never failing to keep her eyes focused on Captain Stransky.

"OK. You can go for now."

Stransky was tired and was no closer to the truth. They had no evidence against the women except the circumstantial evidence of Anne's presence at both events. They had no proof whatsoever. His only hope was that the ranch worker, Jonathan would crack but he didn't. He was very strong and secure under interrogation. The fact that he had resigned his position could not be linked as a motive. The resignation letter to his boss and his boss's reply were very cordial showing no hint of malice on either side. It seemed that the deaths and his resignation were simply coincidental. Even though Johnathan was looking to join "the other side" he did not seem to have caused any friction. Jonathan had simply found a better paid job that would make use of his talents.

Could it be that two middle-class ladies from as far apart as England and America had formed an alliance with a member of staff in the centre? It seemed unlikely but if it wasn't them who was it? Who had sent the death threats? Could it possibly be that these two women had killed an entire hunting party? The American had skills with a gun but the Brit had no training whatsoever. One person couldn't have killed them all.

The fact was Stransky had no hard evidence and no reason to detain them any longer.

CHAPTER 42

The following day Anne and Rachel began the journey home. Jonathan had agreed to drive them to the airport. As they began the slow climb up the track that would take the ranch out of view, they both simultaneously looked out of the rear window.

Anne took a last view of the ranch and fixed it in her mind.

She turned to Rachel.

"No regrets?"

"No, no regrets. No sense of guilt either. They deserved it. I have one doubt though."

"What's that?"

"What if it doesn't change anything? After this ending what if nothing changes?"

Anne turned to her and smiled. It will change things. Next week we are putting out an announcement claiming responsibility for the deaths and explaining the reasons why. There will be more. This is only the start.

"Really? I don't think I could go through that again."

" No. I didn't expect you to. I appreciate all you did."

They embraced and as they did so the beautiful land on which they had attempted to change the world, albeit by one small act, disappeared from view.

Two hours later Johnathan was unloading their luggage in the car park at Polokwane airport. His huge frame towered above them as he looked down fondly at them.

"So much strength and bravery," he thought to himself.

"I'll say goodbye here," he said, "I don't like airports that much. Too much hustle and bustle."

Anne hugged him. "Thank you for all your help and good luck in your new job."

"Thank you. I hope it will be of more use than what I have been doing."

"I'm sure it will be." terminals for leaving South Africa. Anne had a two hour wait whilst Rachel had a little more.

The two women stopped and faced each other.

Neither knew what to say. Rachel broke the silence. "We must keep in touch."

"Absolutely. Friends forever." Anne grinned but she was uncertain. She admired Rachel's courage but was fully aware that she had struggled with her conscience. She understood that part of her anger had been caused by the death of her family in such a tragic way. She had been very brave and sincere but was this the parting of the ways? Their friendship had been intense and focused. Would it survive a return to normality, whatever that meant? Perhaps Rachel would return to her journalism and campaigning.

Anne wondered what normality would mean for her. Would it even exist? Did she want it to exist? She couldn't be involved in a repeat action. Her involvement would become an obvious link. Perhaps the singularity of their action had been its strength. Hopefully a process of change had begun as a result. Whatever the future held she wouldn't be still. The world needed changing and she couldn't rest after all she had been through.

After all the tension and fear and it had to be said, excitement, their parting was quick and normal. They appeared like two friends who had shared a holiday together and were now going their separate ways.
Anne was gone and Rachel prepared for her boarding. The plane took off in the late evening and she managed to capture one last view of the vastness and beauty of this wonderful land before darkness fell. She fell asleep almost immediately as exhaustion overcame her and woke again as the pilot announced the preparations for landing at Heathrow.
It was a pleasant, late March morning in London as her taxi drove her through the post rush hour traffic. London was too busy for the gentle daffodils and seemed to overpower them.
"Been on holiday?" asked the driver.
"I've been visiting old friends in South Africa."

"Oh nice, very nice. Were you near the shootings?" he asked.

"What shootings?" Rachel was stunned.

"Some terrorists shot a bunch of hunters dead. It caused a right stir. It's been all over the news here. They voted in Parliament to stop the import of trophies and pelts. That was going to happen anyway but then this. There's been loads of debate about hunting."

"No. I've been very busy and living on a ranch in the middle of nowhere."

"Well, you're best not knowing I suppose. It just upsets people. I mean I don't agree with hunting at all and I wouldn't buy a fur for the missus even if I could afford one but shooting people. It's a bit extreme isn't it? It's not going to change anything is it?"

"I suppose not." Rachel hadn't got the energy or will to argue. She had doubted whether their actions would change anything. Now she learned they had drawn worldwide attention. Maybe it had been worthwhile after all. She was confused and weary.

"Anyway, we've got our own problems, what with all the strikes and everything."

"What strikes?"

"Cor you have had a good time, haven't you? They've been going on for weeks now. Mainly public sector

workers. They are even talking about a general strike. I don't blame 'em. I mean what the nurses and ambulance workers and others did for us during Covid. They looked after us didn't they? My missus' dad died 'cos of that. Yeah, I don't blame 'em. There's a big demonstration this weekend. I don't think this Government will last much longer if you ask me."
"Really, is it as bad as that?"
"They ought to shoot some of those politicians except it wouldn't make much difference."
These last words hit Rachel. She had been angered about man's cruelty to animals and his fellow beings. She had desperately wanted to do something to stop it and had been motivated into doing an extreme act that she would never have believed herself capable of. Then she had been disturbed by her own actions.
Now the vision of these strikes and protests brought her doubts into focus. Had she done the right thing? Would it achieve her aims? How do you change things? She was deeply troubled. The taxi pulled up outside her house. Rachel exited and paid her fare. The front garden, though small, was alive with spring. She paused for a minute. Andrew had been the keener gardener of the two. She held a brief vision of his face. She could see him kneeling to plant bulbs in a time when life had been simpler. She

sighed before opening the front door and stepped into her loneliness.

Rachel went through to the kitchen. It seemed different or maybe it was she who had changed. So much had happened. She made herself a welcoming cup of tea, sat down at the table, cup in hand and listened to the silence. Normal? What was normal? Life would never be the same again.

She put her head into her hands and sobbed.

THE END

Other Books by this author

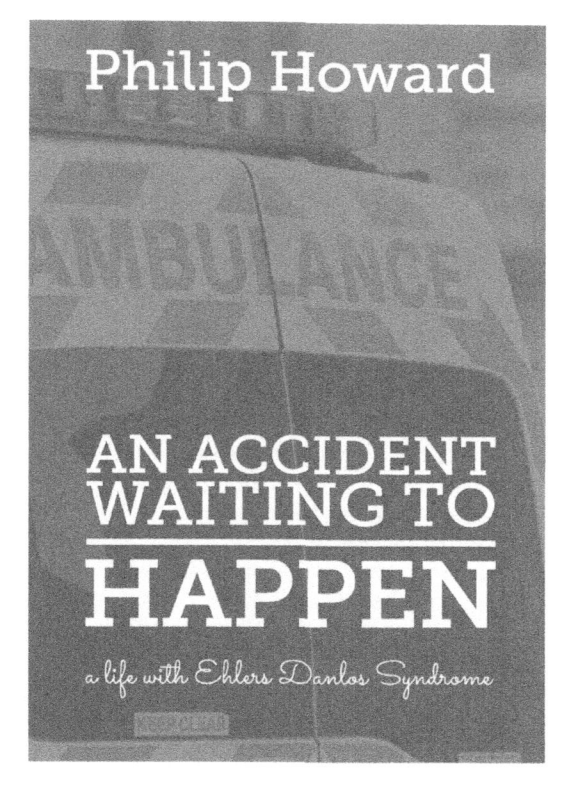

Philip Howard

AN ACCIDENT WAITING TO HAPPEN

a life with Ehlers Danlos Syndrome

Available from Amazon

Braver than all the rest
A mother fights for her son

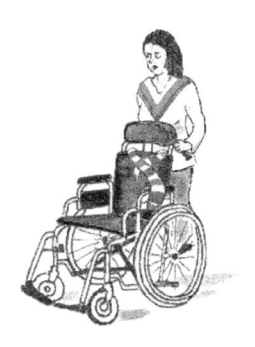

Philip Howard

Dave and Sarah Burgess are devastated when their young son Karl is found to have muscular dystrophy. Then another tragedy hits the family hard. But the family are committed to do the best they can for Karl, who has a passion for rugby league.
Based in Castleton, a Yorkshire town near the border with Lancashire, Karl's determination to get the most out of life, despite his disability, inspires those around him, in particular Chris Anderton, one of the Castleton Rugby League Club players, who is coming to the end of his career in the game.

A paperback version of this book can be obtained directly from the publisher (https://llpshop.co.uk) or from amazon. An E- edition for Kindle readers is available for this book on the Amazon.co.uk website. We cannot supply the E-Book version, please order from Amazon

Printed in Great Britain
by Amazon